Chicago
Story

Marvin Thomas

ISBN: 978-1-4907-4052-2 (sc)
ISBN: 978-1-4907-4051-5 (e)

Trafford rev. 07/18/2014

Trafford
PUBLISHING® www.trafford.com
North America & international
toll-free: 1 888 232 4444 (USA & Canada)
fax: 812 355 4082

CHAPTER ONE

He had forgotten had cold and biting the wind could be in the midst of Winter in Chicago. It blew off Lake Michigan in undulating sheets and drove right to your core. Why he wanted to return at this time of year remained somewhat of a puzzle but perhaps he wanted to relive the impact all of this had on his life. The cold seemed to add the appropriate exclamation point. He had adjusted to the heat of the desert, his new home sufficiently that the cold seemed so much a stranger now, A stranger from so long ago but now his old friend again.

He crossed over to the bus that would take him to the rental car lot. God, I have forgotten how cold it can be here, he thought. All around him, people seemed intent on getting to somewhere warm as quickly as possible. He had brought the only cold-weather item he could find, a trench coat with lining that he had somehow saved from his time here. It was adequate but really not sufficient. He had used the airport many times in his time here and the instant recognition of its solid structure brought a slight smile to his lips.

1

He boarded the bus, put his slim suitcase on the shelf, waited for the bus to fill up a bit more and felt the motor purr as they moved on. He glanced around him. Directly across was a young woman and her husband or boy-friend he guessed. She was quite attractive and he thought she kept looking and smiling at him. He knew he had aged but he also knew he was still a very handsome man. Maybe that played a role in what happened here.

He followed the young woman and man off the bus and headed to his rental car. It was red, of course, red, mid-sized sedan. He thought about renting a sport car like he now had but had decided against it at this time of the year in Chicago. Even the short walk from the bus to the car notified him of the cold. Had he become so unaccustomed to this? Perhaps.

Turning the key, he hoped it would easily start. He remembered the toll the cold could take even on machines. But it did with only a wisp of hesitation Driving out of the airport, he melded into the midday traffic. The skyline of city passed on both sides. He felt the comfort of immediate recognition. Funny, he still had the image of that woman on the bus with him. She was rather beautiful. In another time, oh well, in another time. This was not the mission he was on. Forget it, he told himself. It did not take long for him to get to the Courthouse. Stopping in front of that magnificent looking building, he wanted to carve its image into his brain but he had to move on and so he found a parking lot only a block away.

The wind seemed even stronger here. He thought the buildings would shield him but they didn't. He shivered again and turned the collar on his coat as high as he could. Walking along the street towards the building, everyone else seemed to be just as intent in getting to someplace out of the wind and cold. He opened the large door in front of the building and entered. Why do all these courthouse building seemed to be carved out of the same mold? The floors are hard and unforgiving and the walls built with such a solid feel. But this one seemed even more characteristic than any other he had seen or been in. Marble columns guarded the doors of each room and those doors seemed made of such sturdy wood as to be impenetrable. It had been over ten years since he was last here but he would never forget just where THAT room was located. He climbed the stairs at the end of the hall, again made of solid marble and used to such an extent that even this eternal material seemed to be showing its age.

Surprised at the small number of people in the building, he hoped the room would not be in use and that it even would be open. Room number 220. It was so etched into his memory that just by viewing the numerals, a wave of scenes washed into his mind. He grabbed the handles and with a feeling of relief was able to open them. It was not being used, thank God. He swiftly surveyed its contents. The jury box, now empty, held so much of his attention during those grueling two weeks. He retrieved a facsimile of each of their faces almost instantly. That was how intense their presence was at the time. The bench behind which that judge sat looked as imposing in this empty room as it did then. God, he remembered that judge! George Timms. Yes, that was his name. One of the upcoming stars in the Chicago judicial system. He could still see the image of his etched face, Romanesque with sharp features. A full mane of flowing wavy blond hair and oh, those piercing eyes. He still shuddered a the thought of him After the trial, Judge Timms had moved on to become Chief Justice of the Illinois Supreme Court. He thought he had even been nominated for a federal judgeship but somehow he had lost track, perhaps intentionally, of his course.

He had been one of the most prominent cardiac surgeons in the city. He had graduated from a prestigious Ivy League Medical School in the top ten-percent of his class. He had stayed in the East to complete part of his post-graduate training then moved on to complete it at one of the top Thoracic Surgery programs in Chicago. He had been born and raised in the Mid-west so when the offer to join the most admired Thoracic Surgery group in the city came, he almost instantly accepted it. He was busy almost from the start. He had an appointment at one of Chicago's top teaching hospitals. Brilliant and handsome. and personable he soon became one of the most eligible bachelors in Chicago. He dated frequently, had ample sex, but still ended up marrying his high-school girlfriend. And then it happened.

He let himself drift back, having resisted those thoughts as best as he could until now, to the first time he had met them. She had been referred by one of the cardiologists whom. he knew well and respected. George Cooper was his name He was the senior partner of a group of ten cardiologists who practiced at several of the hospitals that he did. In addition, one of George's junior partners had been a classmate of his in medical school and he had been with him socially on several occasions. He had married his nurse. A lovely woman who was outgoing and cordial and

4

he had enjoyed being with both of them. Funny how he thought of them now. He hadn't seen them now in several years. Maybe I should call them while I am in town. No, not yet. Later. Later.

He would never forget her name. Harriet Johnson. She was in her early forties, a very attractive woman She had been bothered with increasing shortness of breath and her cardiologist had sent her to see Frank who had found an aortic valve stenosis. Apparently this was felt to be congenital and told her and her husband that he felt a surgical repair would be the best approach, given the nature of her problem.

He had gone through the routine initial office visit, obtaining a history of her problem and the need to examine her. He had assumed this had been done before, obviously, by at least Dr. Cooper. She seemed a bit hesitant, although he could not guess why. Perhaps a normal degree of shyness for her. Sensing a possible problem, he had asked his nurse to be present in the examining room with him. She had put on a cloth mini-gown that was used for the women to simply expose their chests for cardiac exam. He noticed, in passing and thinking back, no more than that, that she had moderately large but beautifully shaped breasts. She kept trying, in a somewhat annoying manner, to keep the top closed. He was happy he had brought the nurse in with him but went about the auscultation fairly routinely. There was the tell-tale murmur of aortic stenosis. It was rather loud, like waves crashing onto a beach. He had heard that sound many times and could almost predict the severity and outcome by its volume. When he finished, he told her she could dress and he would meet with her and her husband in his consultation room.

"Helen" he asked his nurse "did she seem a little put out by me having her undress for that exam or am I being just a bit too cautious?'

Helen was in her late forties. She was a plain -looking woman but soft and kind in her approach to his patients. She assisted him in surgery and was truly outstanding in that regard. She was a real asset. Married with three children she was a solid family woman, totally committed to her children and husband. There was never a scintilla of sexual attraction between him and her and he liked it that way.

"She did seem a little squeamish about a rather simple thing, I must admit., Dr. Martin. I think you did the right thing by having me in here. Pretty thing, though, wasn't she?" "Was she?" he smiled at her "I guess I didn't really notice"

"Of course you didn't" Helen answered returning his smile.

"Well, maybe I'm too paranoid in this case. Don't know why. I'll try to get over that when I speak with her and her husband."

He met them in his consultation room. He was a man of medium height; surprisingly he was not particularly handsome. Why did that surprise him? Maybe because she was quite beautiful. He had a very serious look upon his face. Too serious he thought.

"Well, Doctor." The man said "what is the verdict? Dr Cooper seemed quite certain that Harriet would require surgery. Is that true?"

Frank thought he seemed too robotic about this. It was his wife, after all, and he seemed to be going about it like this was a business decision.

Yes.,Mr Johnson, I think Dr, Cooper was correct. Your wife has a rather significant t degree of aortic stenosis. She is getting more symptomatic as she told me. I don't think we should wait too much longer."

"What do I need, Dr. Martin? A new valve?" she asked. She seemed so innocent in that moment. Beautiful and innocent.

"Yes. A new valve. We can use either a pig valve which does not require that you take blood thinners for the rest of your life or an artificial one that will."

Mr. Johnson, his first name was Lawrence, seemed to study him carefully. What was he thinking about? Creepy sort of guy, Frank thought.

"We have already talked to a number of other people. Some medical, some not. Harriet and I think we'd prefer the artificial valve. Is that satisfactory?"

"Perfectly, Mr. Johnson. My nurse will talk with you and Mrs Johnson about the scheduling. It is elective but I think we need to move along."

Is it THAT serious, Doctor?'

He did not hesitate to answer him. Frank thought that a direct, very strong, approach was best here.

"Yes."

Lawrence eyed him carefully. Nodded and then smiled. 'Thank you for your frankness, doctor. We will schedule this as soon as possible."

Frank did not think about this again. He saw many patients and scheduled surgery accordingly. He had a very busy practice and was recognized now as one of the top cardio-vascular surgeons in Chicago. The next time he would see her was the day of surgery.

CHAPTER TWO

He did not think at that time that this particular surgical procedure would change his life forever. Nothing seemed unusual that morning. She was the first on the surgical schedule. He lived in Highland Park near Central Park, a short walk to Lake Michigan in a beautiful home with all the amenities. He had married. Fairy tale sort of stuff but he was very much in love with her. He always had his pick of women but he always went back to her. It was a good move. He drove into Evanston to the hospital at Northwestern as he did three times each week. In spite of the annoying traffic, he enjoyed the view along the lake. After parking his car in the Doctor's lot, he walked into the entrance to the surgical suites of the hospital, went to the locker room and changed into his surgical clothes. Routine, very routine. He always ate his breakfast at home, enjoying the quiet time to read the morning newspaper, a habit he loved dearly and would not give up, no matter how early he had to be here or anywhere else. It was his way to prepare for the day ahead. He went through the usual routine, scrubbing his hands thoroughly. Gary Carson happened to be in the surgical area at the same time.

"How's it going, Gary?"

"Not bad at all, Frank Just have a hernia this morning. Should be damn easy. I think I'll easily make my tee time at noon. How about you? I haven't seen you in a while. Where in the fuck have you been?"

Gary was an average general surgeon. One of those jolly fellows who just made it through medical school but were personable enough and a good enough technician to be what he was now. Pleasant but occasionally annoying.

"Christ, Gary, I really have been around. You've been playing too much golf to notice me."

Gary looked at him with his patented smirk.

"Bullshit. Look, we all know you are the hottest CV surgeon this side of Peoria. But, really, ol 'chap, you've got to take some time to unravel a bit, you know."

They both broke out in spontaneous laughter. Funny how that level of tension exists in the surgical suite, Frank, thought. It felt rather good to let some of that out.

"You're right, of course, you asshole" Frank told Gary." I should. Maybe after this case, I'll take a cruise around the world."

"What's up this morn with you, ace? Gary asked

'Well, a bit more routine than a hernia, I guess, An aortic stenotic valve."

"Wow. Man, I get so impressed so easily. Good luck my man, you ain't going to make it to the tee on time."

Frank laughed at that too, As the room started to fill, they went their own way. Gary to the mundane, Frank to the more exotic. Later, Frank would wish he had only to do that hernia that morning.

When he walked into the operating room, the sterile ambience, as always, struck him. You'd think this would all seem routine, he thought, but it was such an artificial world

9

with its ghostly whiteness and singing lights that he always felt he was in a world like no other. She was on the table, still awake, as he went over to her.

"Good morning, Harriet" he said to her in the calmest tone he could muster

She looked up at him. A faint smile on her face. A face that still was quite beautiful even here with no cosmetic enhancement.

"Good morning, Dr. Martin. I hope you are rested and at your best".

Even in this relatively early stage of his career, he had encountered the whole spectrum of patients just prior to their surgery She seemed to be amongst the calmest that he had met. He knew it was a paramount duty of the surgeon to seem calm, confident, and not unhappy at that time. He was certain he had succeeded, up to and including the moment when she drifted off under the influence of the anesthetic.

The operation seemed to be going well. He and his assistant had made the incision and split the sternum and the heart was exposed. She was placed on the heart-lung machine, the metal creature that would assume the role of her pseudo-body. Removing the damaged valve and carefully replacing it with the prosthesis, he turned to his senior resident to suture it in place. This was a practice that was fairly routine amongst his fellow cardiothoracic surgeons and one he had subscribed to over the past few years. He had been the recipient of the same instructional procedure as a senior resident when he was training and he accepted the gesture as part of the maturing process. Kenneth Laser was the resident with him. A very gregarious fellow, Frank thought. Not brilliant, but smart enough to maneuver his way through the labyrinth of surgical training. He seemed quite competent in his technical skills. Competent enough that Frank turned away from the suturing process for what he later remembered to seem like a split second to ask a question of Helen. Turning back to the surgical cone, he asked him if he was finished. "Two more sutures should do it, Dr. Martin"

"Good. Everything secure?" "Yes sir."

He had answered so strongly and with such confidence that Frank didn't give it a second thought. He had worked with Kenneth before and did not doubt his technical abilities. A happy- go -lucky guy he was but that colorful part of his personality was quite pleasing and complemented his surgical ability. Frank thought that was a formula for ultimate success. He never doubted him that morning.

He went through the usual routine as they wrapped up the surgical sequence. Counting sponges, checking her vital signs, coordinating the completion with the anesthesiologist He walked away from the table, confident that all was well.

Walking out of the operating theatre, he stopped in the locker room, said hello to two other surgeons who were lounging there prior to their surgeries and washed his hands thoroughly. Still wearing his surgical green smock, he walked out into the waiting room to meet Lawrence Johnson.

As stern-looking as usual, he got up from his chair the moment he saw Frank.

"I assume everything went well, Dr. Martin?" he asked him before Frank could say anything.

"Yes, Yes. Mr Johnson. It went fine, They are just finishing up now. She will go to the recovery room for a period of time and then we'll move her into her room after that."

"How long until she gets into that room?"

"Probably early this evening."

"Good. I am anxious to see her. Can I go into the recovery too,?" "Yes, in about an hour or so."

"No surprises?"

"None. Her valve was severely compromised. She definitely needed that new one, believe me."

"I do, Dr Martin. I trust you. I'm looking forward to her returning to her usual self."

As he walked away and went back to the surgical area to relax and to get ready for his next case, a simpler placement of a stent in a leg artery, he felt rather comfortable about his confrontation with him. He always expected the worst from that man. He acted rather civil as matter of fact. He smiled for the first time since that surgery started.

CHAPTER THREE

He finished the day in his office seeing rather routine patients, some post-operative one or two new ones and the rest return. Nothing unusual in all of that. Driving back to Highland Park, he enjoyed the passing scenery. Fall was just starting and the trees were starting to change their colors. He loved this time of year. A crispness in the air, the eye pleasing colors painted on the landscape. Life seemed good at that time.

The evening was nothing out of the routine. Carole had decided to cook that night. She was a rather good one Frank thought. The conversation during dinner was tepid, covering the day with her and their two children. Gary, his son was ten, an outgoing boy who excelled in school. His daughter, Terri, was just into first grade but also showing her enthusiasm for learning that pleased both him and Carole. His phone ringing during dinner was not unusual and there was no sense of urgency about this particular one. He reached over to pick it up.

"Hello, this is Dr. Martin" Carole. for some reason, was looking at him at that moment.

She ordinarily simply continued doing whatever she was doing when he received one of his calls, which was not infrequent. But this time, she had never seen the expression on his face that she saw then. She was aware of the descriptive term some use that "they turned white" She thought that was more imagination than reality but it certainly seemed Frank's face did change color

"When? When did this happen? 'he desperately seemed to be imploring whomever he was talking with.

Frank, what is the world is this all about?" Carole asked

"Trouble, sweetheart. May be BIG trouble. The valve replacement this morning. Tough husband. They're telling me she has stroked out. Alive but I don't know much more. This is one I gotta get to."

Frank, what about your residents?"

"Not this one. I have to be there, in person. Sorry kids, but I'll see you tomorrow" he told them as he quickly kissed both, grabbed his coat and headed out to his car in the garage.

It was a typical Mid-western Fall night. Crisp, as the natives would say. A bit of wind coming off the Lake. Ordinarily, Frank would try to savor all of this at this time of year, enjoying the subtle but pleasing change of seasons. But not tonight. He drove the route to the hospital ignoring all of that which is not to be ignored in times of more tranquility.

His mind was dancing with so many thoughts that it all seemed like a blur.

"Jesus" he thought "of all the people to have this happen. What went wrong?"

He drove too fast, he knew that, but he could not help himself. He was very anxious to get into the hospital and see for himself what the situation really was. Why the image of her husband's face kept running through his mind's eye was bothersome. Was he worried more about what that man could do than what was happening to his patient? Well, if so, he would have to deal with that but for now. But for now.

He drove into the hospital parking lot, quickly found a space which was easy at this time and walked quickly inside. He decided not to wear his white coat., He wanted to get to the unit as quickly as possible. He acknowledged several nurses who passed him by and finally arrived at the surgical intensive care unit. Opening the door, he quickly saw her in the second bed. He had seen this picture many times. The tubes surrounding her, the machines with their colorful but daunting panels of information. But this seemed different this time. He didn't really know why that would be the case but there was that image of her husband again and he knew why.

"Hello, Dr Martin" greeted him as he walked to the bedside. It was Betty Linstrom, one of his favorite nurses in the unit and in charge during this shift.

"Betty. How's she doing?"

"Stable now but still we don't know the extent of the brain damage. The neurology resident dropped in but didn't say much."

"Do we know what happened?" he asked

"Her hematocrit dropped very rapidly I guess. Your resident told me they think she bled" "Bled? From where?" he looked at her incredulously, not believing what he was hearing. "The theory I guess, is that it might have been from around the new valve"

"What!" he exclaimed, a look of both surprise and despair on his face.

His mind was a kaleidoscope of thoughts and emotions. How could that happen? I almost… Jesus! I let Laser finish! How in the hell could he screw up something simple like that? Well, that's for later. Now, let's just get this fucking thing under control.

He walked over and looked at her chart. Her vitals were indeed stable but she was obviously in a coma. Just what was the damage?

"Betty, let's get Dr. Jewel down here if we can. I know it's night and I know his resident saw her but this is critical. If you need me to talk to him let me know. Is Mr. Johnson around here?"

"I think so, Dr. Martin. He was in here not long ago. Told me he would be in the waiting room if he was needed."

"Thanks. I need to see him. Betty, I'm glad you're here tonight.' Thank you very much. I… really appreciate that"

He walked with some degree of trepidation towards the Intensive Care waiting room. He walked past three other beds that were filled with other casualties of medicine's ongoing war. Usually quite confident and satisfied with his world, he did not have that feeling now. The hallway leading to the waiting room was bathed in shadows from the adequate but meager lighting at this time of night. Why did he feel so damn uncomfortable. He hadn't felt like this for years. Opening the door, there was only him sitting in a chair by a dim light, reading something.

"Hello, Mr. Johnson." He addressed him matter-of factly as one does when attempting to pacify a potentially difficult moment.

Frank had never seen the sternness on his face as he showed him that night. His foreboding just grew more intense.

"Dr. Martin. How is she?"

"She certainly appears to be stable. I've asked my consulting neurologist to come in and see her tonight to give us a better handle on this."

"What happened, Dr. Martin? You told me after the surgery that all went well."

"It did. I'm not sure yet what this is all about. That's one of the reasons I've asked the neurologist to give me a hand."

"Will she die?"

"I really believe there is no danger of that at this point. As I said, she seems stable. All her vital signs are good. The real question is her neurological status and as I said, I've asked a really top-notch neurologist to come in as soon as he can to examine your wife." He looked intently at him. That molded stern face did not change its expression... But I just told him I thought she would live. Why does he not show some, just a bit, of relief. This guy bothers me. He really does.

"Well, then, when will this so-called 'top-notch' neurologist be in? It's almost mid night."

"The nurse in the Unit just called him. I expect him, to be here shortly. I'm not certain how far away he lives from here."

"I expect a full report tonight, Dr. Martin"

"Of course, Mr. Johnson. I'll be back just as soon as I know more. I'm confident things will be alright."

As he told him that, he really wasn't sure that she would be alright.

He turned and walked out of the waiting room. He was relieved that his encounter with than man was at least over for now. Frank just had never really met a person quite like that. He didn't know just what it was that bothered him the most: his steely look, his formal tone of voice or just his general demeanor. But he didn't like him and that was foreboding The hall between the visiting room and the Intensive Care Unit was only twenty yards or so but at this time of night it held an eerie feel to it. The shadows from Frank. He had walked this hall a number of times in the past, some even at night, like this, but he never had the visual picture that it presented now. This is weird, he thought. Why am I so damn hung up over this?

He walked back into the Unit. Nothing seemed to have changed since he left it. He remembered the days in training when these units were more open with beds lined up in rows. Now, each patient had their own space, if not their own closed room. But the ambience, the cloud that always seemed to float above these rooms, remained essentially the same. It was a true "battleground" of medicine with the specter of split-second decisions that really did mean, more often than not, the difference between life and death.

When he walked back to see Mrs. Johnson, Ted Jewell was looking at her chart. "God, I', glad you could get here, Ted. I'm really concerned about this case. I'm sorry you had to make a trip in but I would not have called you if I didn't think I needed you now."
Ted Jewell was one of the smartest men Frank had ever met. He was a true intellectual with wide interests… He had trained at Yale and could have stayed on staff there but his mother was not in good health and lived near Chicago and he felt her needed to return. While he had considered life in an academic setting, he chose to go into private practice but accepted the position of Chief of Neurology at this hospital. He had built a fairly strong program and had

two fellows working with him and the other three doctors in his practice.

"No problem, Frank Betty told me how concerned you were".

"Have you had a chance to look things over yet? Any ideas?"

Ted Jewell was rather tall and quite thin. He had a handsome face that did not seem to fit with the rest of his body. He wore glasses that always seemed to fall to the end of his nose and he looked at you over them more often than not. He seemed more avuncular than he actually was but spoke in slow, measured terms. But he was the best neurologist Frank had ever known, including those at his medical school.

"I think she did leak around that valve replacement. I would guess there was enough turbulence and slowing for a clot to form which was sent flying into her head with this result…"

"But it had to be a rather large clot don't you think, Ted, to cause this much apparent neurological damage. I mean she's in a come for Christ's sake."

"I grant you it must have been that. But she does have a loud murmur that she should not have after that surgery."

Frank had not yet examined her. In his somewhat hurried approach after arriving at the hospital, he had simply talked to Betty and quickly looked at her chart. It was that thought of her husband that changed his usual careful approach to things medical perhaps. He looked at Ted and moved over to the cart. She was obviously still in a coma. But she still looked beautiful. He opened her gown. Her chest was covered with a coating of bandages from the surgery. He borrowed Betty's stethoscope and listened. Sure enough, there was that swooshing sound characteristic of blood rushing through a valve that should have been closed but was not. He felt a hint of perspiration on his head, a slight t trembling of his hands. What the hell was this affecting him so much, he thought. He had had unexpected complications following surgery before but it had not affected him quite like this was doing... Once again the brief flashing vision of her husband.

He looked at Ted. Realizing what he had heard meant., he felt a strange sense of helplessness.

"No question about it, Ted. I should not be hearing that"

"I know what your next question is. I think she will survive but I'm just not certain how much residual there is going to be. We should know in a week or two."

"Thanks Ted. I guess. Listen, I do appreciate you coming in. I'll have to tell her husband as best I can. I..." he stopped almost in mid-sentence. Betty's eyes were riveted on him and he knew that he had to be careful what he said. He trusted her implicitly and she was very competent in what she did but he now realized he was thinking malpractice as much as anything and under oath, she would be obligated to tell anything she had heard from him.

He stepped over to the cart once more. He felt that unpleasant sensation once again. This was the first time in his professional life that he had profoundly accepted the fact that there was going to be a legal problem with one of his patients. Did that Laser screw this up? Everything seemed to be going as planned when he had finished his part in the procedure. How could a guy who seems so good fuck up that last thing. Surgery 101.

The walk back to the waiting room almost seemed to be a microcosm of his life until that point. He had done all the right things, he felt, to be where he was now. Studied hard, kept his goal consistently in front of him, and had seemingl y married well with two kids that seemed to fit the acceptable mold of what was an acceptable life-style and practice. Frank, for Christ's sake, why are you thinking like this? It really isn't the end of the world. He hasn't sued you yet. Why are so sure he will?

Nothing had changed when he entered the room but everything had changed. That indescribable face of his seemed to be like a crystal ball to the future. He almost felt his hands trembling. Did her husband represent all the things in one's life that surprise and threaten us?

"Hello, again, Dr. Martin. Did you talk to the neurologist?" "Yes."
"And…"
"I think she has had a clot that got to her brain. She has had a stroke. Dr. Jewell does not think she will die but might have some residual from this."
"What does that mean, residual?" his small dark brown eyes were riveted on Frank. His expression never seemed to change. He was so business-like about all of this. Does he ever get excited, he thought.
"She may not recover all of her previous functioning. It is possible she will be handicapped."
"How handicapped?"
"Mr Johnson, I really cannot say at this time. No one can. We are never certain how much brain function will return following a stroke."
"Dr Martin, I am very disappointed in you. We were sent to you by our cardiologist because he said you were one of the top heart surgeons in the city, And now… you tell me my wife may not… she might end up a vegetable!" he had raised his voice to a level that Frank had not heard before.

And there was just the hint of tears on his face. Well, Frank thought, this guy isn't a robot after all.

"Believe me, Mr. Johnson; I am just as upset about this as you are. I'm not sure why this happened but all of us will do everything our power to speed her recovery as best we can."

"That is to be expected, Dr. Martin. I hope you are right. I may seem like I have a lot of self-control but believe me I am boiling inside."

Frank was uncertain how to approach this. It really was the first time in his career, albeit a relatively short one at this point, that he had felt almost immediately a case could be a legal as well as a medical problem. While he was in a rather high risk specialty, he had not yet faced a malpractice suit. Whoa, Frank, he told himself. You are really getting ahead of yourself. Be steady and calm and work with this guy. He is a jerk for sure but he is her husband and I can understand his concern and anger. As a matter of fact, I also am angry about this. It was then that he began to get that feeling, one that he had heard of. Other doctors who had been sued told him how, no matter what the merits or demerits of the case, it starts to grind on your self-confidence. You know you are no different than before the whole thing began but it makes you think you are "different" Again, he told himself to quit thinking like this. It was more important to be helpful in the management of this patient and not to let these thoughts and by juxtaposition, not let her husband intimidate him at this point.

"I can understand that, Mr. Johnson" he told him before he let "everything m our power will be done. Our staff will keep you informed, believe me."

"Thank you. I do appreciate that. Dr. Martin and I think you will"

With that, Frank left him and went back into the Unit for the final time before leaving the hospital. He had spoke with Betty and was certain that she and the resident staff were on the same wave length with the recommendations of Dr. Jewell. He felt better as he left, less worried that he might be sued and more concerned that she would not only survive but recover a good part of her function. The drive back home was less tense and he even gave himself the luxury of turning on some of his favorite music and humming along with it. Arriving home in the middle of the night wasn't unusual for him but this time his wife was wakened when he came into their room, something that often did not happen. He took a few minutes to explain what the problem was but decided to avoid the concern he felt about that Mr. Johnson. He convinced himself that he worried about this for nothing and he was able to fall asleep much easier than he had anticipated.

Chapter Four

Luckily, he was only in his office the next day to see post-operative and follow-up patients, no surgery being planned on Thursdays. He always welcomed this day for a little "rest and relaxation". Even though he enjoyed the surgery and was devoted to it, he enjoyed this part of his practice. It placed him more in the face to face situations that he had savored during his medical school days and had, at one time, led him to consider a career in Internal Medicine, rather than surgery But he was a bit too mechanistic he thought and perhaps a bit too impatient for the slog of the more drawn out process of the non-surgical disciplines. Still, he enjoyed this aspect and this day.

Another bonus, he thought, was the chance to have breakfast with his wife, and during the school season, with his children. Otherwise he always ate at the hospital, primarily for the sake of time and efficiency. He had heard more often than he wanted the stories of neglect by busy doctors, particularly surgeons, and the havoc that would raise in their personal lives with their spouses and children. He tried to make it a point to spend adequate time with them, both because of that concern and also, because he wanted to and enjoyed it and often regretted the need to spend as much time away from them as he did. He knew that the younger surgeons were quite interested in their time off and their need to be with their families. He appreciated that but also knew that this way of life was just that and a hard taskmaster and doing both right required an enormous amount of dedication.

"Frank did you fix whatever was wrong last night? I know you came in a bit later than I thought you ordinarily do last night." Carole inquired as she laid the plate of eggs and bacon in front of him. These, Frank thought, were so far superior to that he had had in the hospital cafeteria that he wondered why he didn't do this stuff at home more frequently. "Not quite but soon, I hope. It was a patient who had a valve replacement. I think the resident may have screwed things up a bit."

"How could he do that?" Carole's eyes narrowed and a look of concern captured her face, which Frank thought, was as beautiful as face of any woman that he ever seen "I'm not sure yet but I think he didn't fasten the valve as securel y as he should have." "What happens then, Dad" his son, Tim, inquired. Tim was a very bright and considerate boy who seemed cut out of the mold of his mother, disciplined and thoughtful. He was only twelve but Frank kept hoping that these traits would not be sabotaged as he got older and more worldly.

"Well. It seemed that a clot formed and traveled to her brain. She had what looks like a stroke."

"A stroke?" Carole repeated inquisitively

"Yeh. She's really not doing that well. In the surgical intensive care unit, of course. Hopefully, she'll recover a good part of her function but I just don't know"

"The resident must feel pretty bad, Dad." Teri, his six-year old inserted. Teri was the image of her mother with a wonderful gregariousness about her. The apple of Frank's eye, for sure.

"He doesn't know yet, at least I think he doesn't know, honey. I'll see him today."

"Don't be too hard on him, Dad." Tim, told him.

Frank didn't know what to think about that. He was really quite angry about all of what had happened. Mistakes are made, he knew, but this was a really simple part of the surgery to screw up.

"I won't, Tim. I was a resident myself in the way distant past, you know."

The drive this morning into his office, which was adjacent to the hospital, seemed so much more serene than the hurried and troubled voyage of the night before. It was a lovely Fall day with the shades on the trees changing into the rainbows Frank always admired. He enjoyed this time of year, the crispness in the air, the hint of coming winter, and above all the magnificent colors of nature. It reassured him of his decision to move back to Mid-west. The emotional trauma he had felt seemed gone now and he looked forward to his day.

After spending the morning seeing his recovering post-operative patients and two new consults concerning possible surgery, he headed over to the hospital for a bite of lunch and to stop into the unit to see how Mrs. Johnson was doing. Walking into the unit had an eerie feeling of de je vu that seemed unnatural. Fortunately she was stable but still had not regained consciousness nor apparent movement of her extremities.

Suddenly, a figure in white moved next to him. It was Ken Laser. Turning to face him, Frank could not help but notice the appearance of apprehension he presented.

"Good morning, Dr. Martin. I was surprised to hear about Mrs. Johnson this morning at surgical rounds. What happened?"

Frank clenched his fist a bit, not wanting to show any unusual anger but perhaps only disappointment. But he was angry. Control of emotions, however, was one of the requirements of being a surgeon and he waited a moment before answering him.

"It looks like she has had a stroke. The theory is something went wrong in surgery" "What… what seemed to go wrong?" he asked, still with that apprehensive face. "I'm not sure yet, but it looks like the valve wasn't secured."

Frank knew that one of the most devastating moments in the life of a surgical, or any medical trainee, is that point when one's confidence crumbles just a bit. That great barrier you have so tediously built around you that protects is no longer impregnable. This was such a moment for young Ken Laser.

"What do you mean? The valve was not secured. Are you saying that I screwed up?"

Ken was a good surgeon and resident and he was not certain what really did occur. There was no way to absolutely prove that he had made a mistake.

"Dr Martin, I am certain that I secured that valve. I've watched you a number of times and I try to duplicate your technique."

"I'm sure you do, Ken. That's what we all do as we learn, right? Look, I don't know what really went wrong. I am not blaming you but if a mistake was made, we'll have to face up to it and get through this. We cannot go back and straighten things out after the fact. You know that as well as I do"

"What do the neurologists say? Any chance for a reasonable recovery?" Ken asked plaintively.

"Just don't know yet. Time will tell us. Listen, her husband is going to be a toughie.

Might be a good idea for you to go the waiting area and introduce yourself, show him how concerned all of us are and that everything that can be done will be. I've more or less done all of that but the more the merrier so the saying goes."

Frank wasn't quite sure how this young doctor would handle this. Probably well, he thought. He seems bright and capable. But he knew what these things do to you early on in your career. But that is part of the story of medicine.

Frank spent the rest of the day, as planned, in the office seeing post-operative patients and consults. While he was always the surgeon, "working with my hands, you know" he did enjoy this aspect of his practice. This was the "cognitive "part of it, as they said. But he did like the one on one rapport and the ability to think through a bit without the pressures of time and precision. He did not hear any more on the condition of Mrs. Johnson but he assumed that the old adage of 'no news is good news' was playing out here. Interestingly, one of the consults he saw that day was a woman, very close in age to Mrs. Johnson,. Also with a valve problem that he concluded needed replacement. He had wondered what he would feel like when this moment came up again., He didn't think it would be this soon but, perhaps he thought, it was best that moment was now. He felt gratified with the manner in which he handled the situation. Just as he had done with the Johnsons, he sat down with the patient and her husband, he a much more personable and attractive man than the formidable Mr. Johnson. He felt calm and confident, as if he had crossed the Rubicon and mastered the enemy, whatever that was. He assisted them in settling on a surgical date and had his office team go through all the details with her.

The rest of the day was pleasant enough and Frank hardly thought about Mrs. Johnson. Before leaving for home, he dropped by in the Intensive Care Unit to find her basically unchanged, but no worse, which he found encouraging. He relayed that information to Mr Johnson who seemed to be establishing a beachhead in the waiting room. The drive home seemed so much more tranquil and he seemed to notice things from his window that he did not notice before. Strange, he thought, but nice.

CHAPTER FIVE

The next few weeks seemed to proceed in the rhythm that everyday life assumes for all of us. Frank did his usual number of surgeries. That included the valve repair that eerily resembled that of Mrs. Johnson It went quite well with no unexpected events. He did not blink at Ken assisting him at that one and thought he did quite well. He did, however, watch carefully at what he did, particularly at the completion of the procedure. Ken was obviously nervous with it but did not make any mistakes. Frank had thought that was the mark of a maturing surgeon. He continued to visit Mrs. Johnson every day. She was awake now but could not move her right side at all and was unable to ambulate. Her speech had been affected and she had great difficulty communicating. He also saw her husband daily, established in his cove in the waiting room. He grew more difficult by the day and was growing angrier as the time passed. Frank couldn't say he blamed him but there wasn't a thing he could do. The neurologist grew more pessimistic by the day in terms of her recovering any more function. By now, Frank had adjusted to the fact that this was the 'way it was' and he would live with it and continue with the requirements of his life.

She had been removed from the Intensive Care Unit and went into the Neurology Service. Frank still visited her almost every day before leaving the hospital. She recognized him now but certainly had difficulty with her speech which was a bit annoying to him for some strange reason and very bothersome, as expected, to her husband who had taken up quasi-residence in her room. Frank certainly felt, in spite of his vexatious personality, some certain degree of empathy with him. He, after all, was also married and knew how something like this would be absolutely devastating to him should that have happened to his wife. They seemed to have attained a certain level of civility about the situation but Frank doubted if he had accepted what had occurred and her present state. Since there were doubts about future improvement, it had been decided, reluctantly by Mr. Johnson, to send her to a nursing home setting to further acclimatize her and him, actually, to the way life was going to be. She could speak a bit but not well and could not walk without assistance. It was hoped that part might be improved with physical therapy which could be administered in the setting of a nursing facility. Frank had made time in his schedule to visit with her the morning of her discharge.

The room that she occupied was one of the more ample ones in size and well decorated in the hospital. Frank had seen to it that she would be given that room. Whether her husband was impressed with that gesture was unknown but he had made sure, in subtle ways, to make certain he knew what Frank's role had been in securing it for her. It was a sunny day and the light flowed in through the ample window exposure, making the area more cheery than Frank imagined it was for them. Standing in the room was

Mr. Johnson, perhaps with less of that gaze that projected danger.

"Nice of you to drop by, Dr. Martin "Frank could never identify the emotion behind much of what he said to him.

"I did want to wish you both the best. Hopefully, things will improve."

He was careful not to make any promises and hesitated to apologize for what had happened. While intuitively he knew that might be helpful with his rapport, he just did not trust this man.

"Thank you, Dr. Martin. I'm sure you did the best you could but obviously, we are both a bit disappointed"

"Believe me, so am I." Frank countered.

"I assume you have taken steps to insure that something like this won't happen again." He studied that face again, the narrow eyes and the slim lips that seemed to always maintain the probable evolution into a grin.

"Lawrence" he invoked his first name, the first time he had done that since the incident occurred. "we always take measures to try to avoid problems." "For yourself and the patient I assume"

Frank did not answer directly but simply nodded his head and left it at that.

He walked over to the chair where Harriet sat. She was still beautiful and still so innocent but now like a magnificent painting with interposed blank areas. Medicine was a rewarding and fulfilling way to spend one's life but it was times like this that can cause such countervailing agony. She seemed able to comprehend what one was saying but had great difficulty in articulating a response He looked at her as if she was his wife or child. He felt so bad about it all and at times like this wanted to strangle that resident but knew he would have felt just as badly in this scene.

"Mrs. Johnson, Harriet, I want to wish you the absolute best. I am still confident things will get better." That, Frank knew, was half hope and half fantasy. But that was what a doctor does and all he could do under these circumstances.

She nodded and held her hand out take his. Tears barely perceptible but accumulating, struck Frank in a way that was making this scene too tense and uncomfortable for him. He said good-bye again, shook Mr. Johnson's hand and walked out the door.

CHAPTER SIX

Surprisingly, he had managed to almost, not completely, but almost forget about Mr. and Mrs. Thompson. During the next several months, his life returned to normal. He continued to do his usual number of surgeries and had not had any complications Kenneth Laser had assisted him on several of those surgeries and, as Frank had hoped, had learned from what may or may not have been a mistake during Mrs. Thompson's case. His private life was settling down again and he and Carole had arranged on several occasions to get away for dinner and often a movie. Frank was an inveterate movie lover and liked the escape into the fantasy life of the screen. It was so different from the fast paced and demanding character of his surgical life. Carole enjoyed being out with him and even liked the frequent stares he would get from other women. Frank was definitely handsome enough to be on the screen himself. She found that sexually stimulating and they found the time to have sex at lest twice a week, sometimes more. Frank found this to be supportive in his attempt to balance his life with his work and thought she was quite good in bed.

That first ominous feeling came on a routine day he was seeing post-operative patients in his office. He was at the end of his schedule and, as was his habit, took time to open his mail. While he often took that home if time did not permit its attention during the day, he preferred not to so as to give more time to his family. He took a second look at the return address on one of envelopes. It was marked 'Stanley J. Edwards, Attorney-at-Law 'Frank had received a number of these in the past, often dealing with those who sought disability where more information was needed. But, there was something about this envelope that seemed different. All of us have these experiences in our daily lives where a routine matter seems not so routine for inexplicable reasons Opening it, he took. one glance and felt that first rush of anxiety that one feels at times of foreboding. It was a request for his records concerning one 'Mrs. Harriet Johnson' He laid the letter on his table and for a few moments simply stared out into the walls surrounding him. He knew, or at least he thought he knew, what all of this meant. Strange. All throughout the time of her surgery and her subsequent hospitalization, he had been concerned about a law suit. And, for some strange reason, after what he thought was a rather cordial encounter the day of her discharge, he had, more or less, felt more and more comfortable about it and had actually not thought of the possibility for the past month. Actually, this was the first time that he had faced a possible law-suit. He knew that this was the 'cost of business', that law-suits were not uncommon, particularly with surgeons, and particularly with those in relatively high-risk specialties, such as his. But, it had never happened to him. Until now.

'Maybe this is just exploratory and after reviewing the information, no suit will be filed' he thought. He knew this was a bit of rationalization on his part. Almost certainly, that will not be the case and he will be sued. Frank sat down in the chair of his office and closed the door. He didn't want to fall behind on his schedule but he felt deflated. He knew that he was an excellent surgeon. Didn't everyone tell him that? Hadn't he had supreme confidence in his own ability? Of course. Why did this bother him so? He knew this happens to many doctors. Again, the 'price of business;' he had been told. Why he thought he was beyond the reach of this web he did not know. Besides, it really wasn't his fault. It was that resident that may have made the mistake. Will he be involved if this indeed goes to trial.? Somehow, that did not help him. He couldn't shake off this feeling of disruption in his life.

The rest of the day was difficult. He was not his usual vibrant self, relishing the face-to-face patient encounters. He hoped none of them would notice but he was sure they had. But he was careful to do what was necessary and not let this obfuscate what he needed to do with each of them. But he was glad when the day ended. The office staff did not say anything to him as he finished his last patient which reassured him to some extent that he hadn't.

The drive home that evening was rather melancholy. He went over the surgery again and knew that it was NOT his fault It was that damn resident who was negligent if there is any negligence here. He knew that there probably was but he was playing the mind games that he later realized most surgeons do under these circumstances. It was late in the Fall and he ordinarily loved this time of the year in the Mid-west. The rainbow of colors embracing the trees always gave him an euphoric visual rush. But not so much tonight.

Dinner was not that unusual but he knew that Carol suspected something was not quite right by her mannerisms and sly glances. Strange how marriage seems to implant the receptors for those signals that men and women direct towards each other. After they had all finished, he had spent the time he cherished with his children, going over their work in school. Whether they noticed his lack of enthusiasm was uncertain but if so, that feeling was not conveyed to him. When both of them had retreated to their rooms, as was the usual routine on a school night, Carole sat down next to him on the big, deep couch which was his favorite "Frank, darling, what happened today. Obviously something is bothering you." "Perceptive little devil, aren't you? Well, I received a request for the records of that Mrs. Johnson that I talked to you about."

"I think so" Carole looked somewhat uncertain.

"Well she's the one who I think the resident may, and I mean may, have screwed up in the closure of a valve repair and she had a neuro event that ;left her rather messed up."

"Oh yeh, honey. I remember. Why?"

"Well, I received a request, from a lawyer, of course, for her records" "Does that mean that they are considering a lawsuit?"

"Certainly looks like it, hon.".

"But, it really wasn't your fault, Frank. Why in the hell would you be sued?

"A suit like this will involve everyone who was in anyway involved and, obviously, I was one who was clearly into that. It doesn't make any real difference, I guess."

"What happens next?'

"Well, I send in all the information that I have. Her lawyer gets it to some doc who looks at this stuff and the decision will be made as to whether to start a suit. Simple as that."

"Simple? Frank, you make it sound like this is sort of. I don't know, a children's game. You've never been sued before. You shouldn't have been now."

"Whoa. Look, Carole. I really haven't been sued yet. Do I think this will come to that?

Yes, I think it will but for now, all I can do is keep doing my thing."

"Honey, is this going to start affecting you? I mean, will it bother you enough to interfere with your practice. You know what I mean."

"I sure as hell hope not"

"You know I will help you in anyway I can" she told him.

Frank drew her close to him and they embraced. Whether that caused some sort of erotic switch to be thrown in her or if this was feminine response to a subconscious cry for help, he did not know. But their sex that night was quite satisfying and eased his mind.

Even though he hadn't been informed in any official way that he was to be sued, Frank had been told to contact his mal-practice carrier whenever there was any hint of it. Whether a request for his files on a patient would qualify as a hint he wasn't sure but suspected that was probably true. His carrier was Midwest Protection. He had been with them for a number of years and since he had not been involved in any suit had encountered no obvious problems. Other surgeons he knew also carried them and he had not heard of problems even the one or two that he had known had been sued. He did know that his premiums had been sharply increasing over the past few years but that seemed to be the situation in the medical liability arena these days. The 'word on the street' was that this was all the 'price of doing business'. After the usual odyssey through the electronic phone system he reached someone who could take his question

"Hello. This is Dr. Frank Martin. I have received a request from a lawyer concerning one of my patients. Am I talking to the right person?"

"Yes" a, high soprano-pitched reply came. "Is that all that has happened at this point?'

"Yes" Frank answered

"Thank you. Just get me the name of the patient and there is not much to do until something more happens."

"That would be a Mrs. Harriet Johnson."

"Harriet Johnson. Is that correct?" "Yes. That's correct"

"Fine. Thank you. Obviously, if you are notified of a pending suit please let us know immediately." the voice concluded.

"So, no more for me to do at this time?" he asked

"No. Really, doctor, this is pretty common to get this kind of inquiry. They send a lot of this stuff on to some 'expert witness', if they can find one, and see if there is any merit in the case. I'm sure you know that lawyers like to take the 'winners' so their reward is worth the effort."

"Thanks. Hopefully, I won't need you."

"Probably not, doctor, but we'll be here for you." The voice concluded. Actually, the voice was that of a female, youngish he speculated, and with a touch of an English accent but he didn't ask where she was. He found that voice calming but still, that foreboding feeling wafted over him again.

He doubted that he would not be sued but, still, why let that interfere with you life at this point he thought. He continued, as he had before, to follow his schedule. He felt comfortable with that even though it did not always follow an exact line. It gave his life structure and, of course, meaning. He did not feel there was any deterioration in his surgical outcomes as he struggled, consciously and unconsciously not to let the prospect of a law suit seep into his marrow. He was surprised how well Ken had gained more confidence each time he assisted him. He was determined not to undermine him. He still couldn't be sure that a mistake had been made although he suspected there may have been. Nevertheless, without the kind of solid proof he would demand of any scientific endeavor, he refused to publicly ostracize him and wanted to be constructive. Ken Laser was very thoughtful with a gift of empathy with his patients. Frank did not want to destroy a talent like that. Besides, he seemed to be a damn good surgeon.

Three weeks later, he received the notification that he was a defendant in a lawsuit filed by Harriet Johnson.

He was not really surprised. He was in his office that day. Whether the notice was to be delivered when he was there in person or not he did not know but it really did not seem to make any difference. The envelope had that official look which always attracts one's attention. He had that shuddering feeling that he knew exactly what it was going to say. He literally tore it open and read it quickly. The suit alleged medical negligence in regards to the surgery involving a Mrs. Harriet Johnson resulting in irrevocable neuralgic deficits.

Years later, he would often reflect on that moment and on that day. He had drifted along with confidence and comfort, actually, over the past several weeks. Why with that piece of paper, he suddenly felt he was an incompetent surgeon and indeed was at fault he couldn't fathom. Yet he knew something did go wrong at the time of that surgery. He suspected it was indeed Ken Laser's error and his not paying attention to that short moment in the procedure. But was that his fault? Would he be an 'accessory' to the crime, so to speak? He had never been sued before and the shock to his feeling of self esteem was more than he thought it would be. He knew he was a good, no, an excellent, surgeon but this... this was making him feel like a goddamn incompetent.

He went through the rest of the day in a state of semi-animation. He forced himself to listen to the patients that he was seeing but his mind seemed like he was switching channels on a television set. He didn't know if his office staff noticed anything different. He looked at them from time to time, making sure he was not deviating from his usual office demeanor and flow. It didn't seem that they were aware of anything different and he did not wish to tell anyone in his office. He still couldn't believe the effect that that innocent piece of paper was having on him. He kept remembering that phrase" it's part of doing business". Why could that not calm him now? In the future, he would look back on that moment and be able to realize that it was, in part, true, 'part of doing business'. But now, it began to grind on him and as the days went on fueled the flames that he could not extinguish. Yes, that little piece of paper seemed to be saying to him, you are an incompetent doctor. You fooled yourself. This will bring you back to earth and restore the appropriate serving of self-doubt that should form a part of your professional life and opinion of yourself.

The drive home that night seemed to be, once again, wrapped in melancholy. He didn't mind the slow pace of the traffic that seemed to engulf him. It gave him more time to think. He turned on some soft music that seemed to help him try to sort out his thoughts. It struck him that he had not called the firm handling his malpractice after just talking to them not long ago. He would do that first thing in the morning. He looked at the flowing cars on the other side of him and realized all were going somewhere. Why should he change his goals and destinations because of this? Easier said than done, as the old saying goes, he thought. But he was determined to continue to play out his life as he always had. Period. This will require taming his emotions, he knew. But he was determined to do it. Do what he had always done. Confront the problem. Face the ball the pitcher had decided to throw at you. He had always succeeded in the past with this attitude and he would do it again.

He finally drove into his garage feeling more confident, at least for the moment. He would not let this peel away that fortress of resolve that was so much a part of him. The familiar surroundings were tranquilizing and as he switched off the motor, he felt a surge of contentment, finally. But that would not last. He openend the garage door and went inside.

"Hi Anyone home,? He asked

"Hi, honey" Carole answered form just off the kitchen which was astride the entry from the garage. "Aren't you home a little early?"

"Yeh, maybe. It's my office day, remember, and I was able to get away a little earlier."

She met him in the hallway. She was, as always, in her even mood which he always found comforting. The fact that she was beautiful didn't hurt either She kissed him and told him how it was always nice when he was able to get home early. But, again with that ingrained perception she had, looked at him with a questioning gaze.

"Frank, honey, what's wrong?"

"What do you mean?"

She smiled a gentle smile that signaled that feminine ability to pierce a man's fayade and get to the very essence.

"C'mon, Frank honey, I know when something is on your mind."

He went to lay his briefcase down in the kitchen as he was prone to do whenever he came from a day at the office but Carole seemed a bit dogged about this.

"C'mon, there is something, isn't there?"

"I am being sued" he answered directly and without emotion. "By that woman?'

"If you mean the one I told you about, that I had to leave that night, and had something to do with my resident, yes."

"How much money is involved?"

Frank was a bit surprised at that question but he didn't know why. Of course, a lot of this was about money. He had been thinking only about his perception of himself.

"I don't know. I. guess I haven't thought that far ahead yet

"Well, isn't hat what's all about, anyway, honey?"

Frank thought this was a microcosm of the kaleidoscope of emotions and ideations about malpractice, For the layman, which obviously his wife was in spite of being married to a doctor, it was more about the amount of money involved. To him, and perhaps, he thought, to most doctors, it was about the affront to their self-perception and ego.

"Yeh, I guess that's what's it's all about. "What happens now?" she asked

"I think I contact my insurance carrier and tell them. I already have. I mean I told them when I received the requests for my records. They told me not to worry. Most of these do not come to fruition. Well, this one sure as hell did."

Carole was a stabilizing influence on him. She had always been. But he wasn't sure she would be much help in this situation She just couldn't fathom the feeling he had. But she moved over to hug him and tell him all would be fine. He was a great doctor and don't most surgeons get sued sometime in their career

"Yes. I guess so. But this is me, honey. This is me."

CHAPTER SEVEN

The next several weeks were as if he was in a dream. He was still having a difficult time adjusting to what was happening. He did contact his insurance company as soon as he received the notice of a law suit. They had informed him of the law firm that was to represent him. Several days later, he received a call from a Mr. Alan Donnaldson who was to be his lawyer. Mr Donnaldson asked if Frank could meet with him soon. A date was arranged on Frank's office day as he thought this would be the easiest to rearrange and not have to cancel any surgeries.

Appropriately, it was a typical cool and cloudy day in Chicago when the meeting was scheduled. Frank had agreed to come into town to his office rather than in the hospital or his place. It was in a large office building, not too; far from the courthouse where a number of law firms seemingly had their headquarters. He admired the lobby of that building, ornate but rather sturdy in its construction. Why do these building always look like this. Glancing on the directory, he found the name of the firm and took the elevator up to the tenth floor. Getting off, Frank realized that the firm must occupy the entire floor for he didn't see any anything else around except that large door that announced the entry. Walking through, the reception area was well designed and bright. It found that appealing. Behind the desk sat a number of women, one of whom addressed him. She was probably the youngest and rather attractive. Frank thought she gave him that little smile that women often gave when meeting a man as handsome as he.

"May I help you, sir?' she asked in a rather seductive way that Frank couldn't ignore. "Well, yes. I'm Dr. Frank Martin and I have a meeting with Mr. Donnaldson."
She glanced at her computer screen"
"Of course, Doctor. Please have a seat for a moment and I'll inform him that you are here."
Frank thanked her and sat down in a chair that seemed too soft and comfortable for just a waiting room item. The trappings of a successful law practice, he thought. The young secretary kept projecting these little smiles at him. He had had plenty of opportunities in the past to team up with other women but he never really gave it that much thought. But he knew his male ego still enjoyed the attention. She suddenly arose from her chair and came out to the waiting room. He should have known better but he seemed to surprised to find that she was merely going to escort him to the office.
"This way, Doctor"
He followed her down a long but brightly lit hall to a door at its end. She certainly had the body that accompanied that face and in his younger, unmarried days. Oh well, forget that. She knocked on the door and when a voice replied to come in, opened it. Frank followed her in. A tall, middle-aged distinguished looking n man with graying hair in an expensive suit with a tie a little too bright moved forward to greet him.

"Good morning, Doctor Martin. I'm Alan Donnaldson. Glad to meet you. Please come and sit down" Thank you Miss Farber, I appreciate your help" With that, the attractive young woman closed the office door and Frank sat down in another chair that was just too comfortable "Now, Doctor, a bit of background. I have been with this firm for twenty years and have devoted most of that time to medical malpractice claims, representing the defendants. I think I have a pretty good track record"

Frank smiled at him. "That is reassuring."

"I hope so. Now, like most doctors that are sued, I suspect you are a bit angry and worried at the same time.".

Frank let that question simmer for a moment. It was, obviously, the type of inquiry you'd expect from someone who had had considerable experience in handling malpractice suits. It was both reassuring and at the same time somewhat condescending.

"You got that one right." Frank thought that was the most inoffensive response. He wanted this relationship to be a good one from the start.

"Well, Dr. Martin, as you may or may not have heard, I have had considerable experience in these matters. You can rest assured I will do everything in my legal power to work this one out for you."

"I appreciate that."

"Good. Now's get started. This is just an exploratory meeting, you understand. More concrete meetings will be needed in the future. I have had chance to review the complaint against you. Allegedly a Mrs. Johnson is accusing you of gross negligence during a surgical procedure that has resulted in what seems to be permanent neurological deficits. Is that correct?"

"Allegedly" Frank answered, somewhat sternly but not in anger. He had been told by several of his colleagues not to let anger get the best of him. That was not a good sign either to his lawyer or, in the future, to the jury. He was angry he admitted to himself but more at his resident than the lawyer or really, himself. The whole set of circumstances was casting such a pale over him and his life. "Dr. Martin. Allegedly is probably what is involved here but it is not the basis to start our professional relationship. There is, indeed, a specific complaint that has been registered against you and the hospital and your associate. That is what we must deal with. Now, can we start from that premise?"

Frank looked at the rather stern face of Mr. Donnaldson. A rather handsome man with features that seemed carved from marble, For some reason, he appeared to Frank what he had always thought a lawyer should look like. Strange feeling that, he thought.

"Of course. You can understand I really do not want to be here."

"I do understand. Most doctors don't. You have the option of settling out of court. It will avoid any of this. But I believe you feel this was not directly your fault, if there is one." "My resident, who was assisting me on this case, does not feel he did anything inappropriate. There was a few moments during that procedure when I did not directly supervise him and what happened may have occurred then but I guess unless we had an autopsy we don't really know what went wrong or if that was really a fault of his. I know it was no fault of mine."

Mr. Donnadson continued to look, Frank still felt sternly was the best way to describe it, at him. He was quiet for a minute or two and Frank was ready to tell him to just say one goddarnn word.

"I was hoping to hear that from you." "What does that mean?" asked Frank.

"You don't want to settle out of court is what that means"

Frank was uncertain if that really meant it was good for him rather than me and this would mean more hours he could chalk up to the insurance carrier. But that was not his problem. His problem was proving to the world that he was as good as he knew he was and this was not his fault. That is what this was all about. He didn't care if this smart son-of-a bitch made his fortune from his case or not.

"No, I don't"

"Good. Now let's get down to particulars. This is just a preliminary meeting, if you will, Dr. Martin. I do have a bit of info here about the case. I just want you to fill in the gaps and I'm sure you will find a bunch of those."

"Fine. Let's get started."

He spent over an hour, more than he thought this might take, in discussing the case with him and offering his additions and subtractions.

"Well, Dr. Martin. It seems to me that your defense rests on two, or maybe more but two I can see now. First, that what happened to Mrs. Johnson was really just a fact of nature, not due to anything that either you or Dr. Laser did. Second, that if there was someone responsible for what happened to her it was Dr. Laser's mistake and not yours."

That candid synopsis sounded coarse and direct and final. It struck him that he was hiding behind the fact that it was indeed Kenneth's fault and not his. Period. He was just too good of a surgeon to be blamed for something like this.

"An astute summary and yeh, that's what I'm thinking,.

"But, Dr. Martin," and this continued formal use of his name was becoming a bit irritating, "Mrs. Johnson was reasonably healthy before that surgery and not so after. An indisputable fact, correct?"

"Correct" Frank promptly responded. He wasn't arguing that nothing had changed just that it was not his fault.

"Well, that fact alone obviously, isn't terribly in our favor" he told Frank somewhat sardonically. "I'll need to consult some of my colleagues and perhaps another cardiac surgeon or two and see how our defense will be formulated. I agree that a this point it would appear our best approach, and perhaps the true one, is to remove the blame from you and place it elsewhere. You will still be implicated but not nearly as severely as say Dr. Laser or nature. Does it bother you that we are attempting to shift any fault to your younger colleague?".

Frank sat a bit immobilized by that question. Down deep he knew that if anything did go wrong, and the facts did speak for themselves in that regard, it was truly Kenneth's and not his doing. But, Ken was a good resident with a bright future ahead of him. What would a verdict primarily aimed at him do to all that? In a flash he had to make a decision between self-preservation and a morsel of altruism.

"No." he finally answered. But it did and he knew it right away. But he was the accomplished surgeon well established now at still a young age in large metropolis. Ken could go anywhere else even if this caused a temporary stain on his resume. Fuck it. I'm know this is the right thing for me.

Donnaldson gave him a look that Frank was not able to peg. Did he think that was too selfish or clever? Well, it's my hide that may be on the line and not his so I really don't care.

"Fine. That may well be the way we proceed but let me do a bit more detective work and pondering and we'll meet again. Now, you know, do not talk about any of this with your colleagues or certainly the plaintiffs attorneys."

"What about my wife?"

"That's your choice, Dr Martin, but I suspect you will and you can." "So, what's the next step in all of this, counselor?" "The trial date is set for six weeks from now. That should give us time to construct our defense. The next step for you will be to meet with the plaintiff attorneys for a more or less formal inquiry. That can, though, be used in court so I'll be with you to advise appropriately."

"When will that be?"

"Soon. I'll be in contact. Well, Dr. Martin, that does it for now. I am aware of your reputation and feel we have an excellent chance of avoiding any damage to that."

Frank smiled a somewhat wan smile and shook his attorney's hand. He had been assigned to defend him by his insurance carrier but he had heard that 'that guy is good. I wouldn't change". So he had not. He was somewhat impressed with his demeanor and bearing. He certainly did project what most would consider a lawyer and the office surrounded you with a feeling of achievement and, certainly, prosperity. Frank felt that must be a good sign but he was still bothered by his decision to veer the spotlight to Ken Laser. He took the drive home, he had not scheduled anything for the day, as he was uncertain about the length of this process. His thoughts seemed to run in opposite directions and that bothered him. He knew, intellectually, that being sued was 'part of the business of medicine' but emotionally it was still enslaving him in the feeling that he was not as good as he knew he was. Bothersome, to say the least. The path he had chosen with Donnaldson still was consuming but, almost as a reaction to that, was his conviction that this just was not his fault and proving that was necessary to restore his equilibrium.

He unlocked the door to his home, a bit quiet yet, with both of his kids in school. The familiar voice of his wife inquiring if he was home already was both comforting and troublesome, What would she think of what had transpire, While he knew she was fiercely loyal to him she still had a steady moral compass that he admired. Neither of them were religious in the sense of church goers but both felt they generally tried to do the 'right thing'.

"hi darling" she addressed him with one of her several affectionate sobriquets. "how did it go?"

Frank took her hand and they kissed with the same degree of passion they shared. He felt comfortable in her embrace, that security they both needed and received from each other. Sitting down at the kitchen table, he went over in some detail his meeting with Alan Donnaldson. He told her how the decision to point the big finger at Ken Laser was troublesome to him but probably the correct approach to his defense.

"I agree that is the way to go" she told him. Her answer surprised him a bit. He thought she would not appreciate his trying to put most of the blame on such a young man. "You're just too good, honey, to do anything wrong in any surgical procedure."

Frank was aware that her love and loyalty was probably shifting her that way but he appreciated her strong support. It helped soften the burden of guilt that he could not evade yet.

CHAPTER EIGHT

He was uncertain if he should discuss his meeting with Donnaldson with Ken Laser. He wasn't even sure if Ken had been included in the suit, although he surmised that he must be. It was unavoidable that he and Ken would be working together as this was his tour with him. Frank was working hard to get his life back on some sort of even plane while he awaited the actual trial to begin. He was aware of the upcoming deposition with the plaintiffs attorneys but that did not seem to be as bothersome as the thought of the trial. He had continued to schedule patients for surgery and he was a bit surprised how he seemed to lose himself in the needs of the moment with each procedure. It surprised but comforted him.

It was two weeks after his meeting with Donnaldson. A aortic valve replacement was scheduled for the morning. It involved a pleasant 70 year old man who had just retired as head of a large insurance company. He was well known in Chicago, one of the movers and shakers. He realized the image he had established as one of the best cardiovascular surgeons in the area still was out there that this man, who could afford to go literally anywhere in the world chose to stay home and sign on with him. And why not, he thought.

He as the best around. Why should anyone want to go elsewhere?. He had never so strongly thought this way :that he was so… so superior. What the fuck? Was he sliding into a state of denial about the possibility that he could make a mistake? Maybe.

.But he was good and he did not make any mistakes. Quit thinking that way, Frank, he told himself. But as so often happens, a opposite thought seemed to glide along parallel was he letting himself get into the state of thinking he as infallible? He knew he never consciously thought that way, this was the reaction to that suit, had to be. A surgeon must never think he is, in fact, infallible.

He met Ken in the doctor's lounge as he was changing from his street clothes into his surgical scrubs.

"Good morning, Doctor Martin." he nodded to him in that subservient way that Frank thought was still appealing these days. But Ken was also a really polite guy which didn't make him feel any better about all of this either.

"Good morning, Ken."

"Nice guy we have this morning"

"Yes, yes, For such a big somebody, he does seem down to earth." "He is having a lot of trouble breathing, he told me."

"Yes, I know. This should do the job. I hope." He noticed his adding the "I hope" part. Odd, that, he thought

They continued to exchange pleasantries and some medical minutiae. He still couldn't bring himself to asking Ken if he had been served notice. But he was sure he had. Finally, Ken stopped talking for a minute and after hanging his head down for a few seconds, looked back at Frank somewhat helplessly.

"Dr Martin" he began slowly. "I received notice that I am being sued by that lady that had a neuro complication."

"I did too, Ken. Have you talked to an attorney? I have been trying to figure out how I would approach this with you. I'm glad you spoke up."

"Uh… no. I… haven't said a word to anyone yet. I… was surprised although I guess I shouldn't have been. I wasn't sure I could get sued as a resident." "You are a licensed physician, Ken. That makes you fair game."

"What did your attorney say? Are they saying that we did something wrong during the operation that caused her to have that problem?"

Frank wanted to just not say anything more. But he felt this keen sense of both guilt and obligation to go on. At the same time, he felt this moment was going to arrive sooner or later. Woven into all of this the reminder he was cementing within that he was just too good of a surgeon to be at fault.

"Ken." Why was he pausing. C'mon, Frank get on with it." :my attorney went through all the crap. Something did happen but he's not certain anyone is really at fault. But he is certain it wasn't me."

There. It was out. Ken, you are a dear fellow. A good surgeon. A… still a great future? But. I'm too good a surgeon.

He waited for the response. Ken'ss eyes seemed to narrow. Was he taking a deep breath? Answer me, goddarnn it.

"Dr. Martin. Are you… he saying… that it was mine then?"

"Ken, I didn't really say that. Remember, he isn't certain that there was any fault, if you will, other than the way nature operates. But, it wasn't my fault.",

"Listen, Dr. Martin. I am not aware that I did anything out of the ordinary. I thought I closed as I've always done with you. I just don't remember any loose ends."

"And there probably wasn't any, Ken. That's my point. We really don't know that anything we did had anything to do with that complication. Obviously, she went into the surgery without them and the temporal relationship, obviously, puts us in a bad light." "Yea. Obviously. But… I think you are inferring that light is going to shine on me." "Ken, as I said, nobody yet is saying they know exactly what happened But we both feel we did not make a mistake. I guess this is all about proving that."

He knew something did go wrong and he was sure it was probably Ken's fault. But, don't box him in. Frank thought he was playing this just about right.

"Ken, as a resident in training, you are covered by the hospital's Master Plan and they will get you to a lawyer that they use, I was just trying to make sure you started the process as soon as you can so not to be caught off guard. Talk to Mr. Leonard in administration. He handles this stuff."

Ken's demeanor seemed to mellow. The anger seemed to evaporate a bit. Good, thought Frank. He is a good kid but… anyway, nothing's been proved yet so let's keep him on an even keel.

The surgery went well. Ken seemed to be solid. He was a bit jovial, even, a bit of a surprise Frank thought but comforting to him. I'm glad that's over. But the shit is yet to come, he thought. And this could be a big fucking mess before it's over.

CHAPTER NINE

Frank felt as if he was floating through his life now. He did not seem anchored as he normally felt and this was distressing. He was as bit obsessive and compulsive. He had recognized that for many years. But, this was an asset as far as he was concerned. Most doctors probably shared that characteristic which probably helped them through medical school. Now, it was the instinctive engine that drove him. The concept of his near infallibility, which he recognized now was a major defense mechanism with this cloud over him, was a bit disturbing but he also felt, genuinely, that he was that good.

He continued to work with Ken without difficulty or animosity. He continued to appreciate Ken's surgical skills, unpolished as they yet were, but still there. Seemingly he had something of a lapse on that day. He learned more about Ken each day. He was the only child of blue-collar parents,. His father was a non-skilled man working on the assembly lines in Detroit. His mother, to help make ends meet, also worked as a cleaning lady. He had been an outstanding student but college would be a major financial challenge to the family, even with some help. Ken managed to work his way through pre med with the help of a church sponsored loan. When he told them he wanted to be a doctor there was no hesitation in their agreement to 'find some way' to finance that.

Frank often detected tears in his eyes when he spoke of them and the sacrifices they had made for him.

It was just after a routine coronary by-pass when in the surgical lounge, that Ken brought up the visit he had had with his lawyer.

"Dr. Martin. I. did meet with a lawyer last week. He is part of the group that works for the carrier our hospital uses. Nice guy, really. About your age." "Yeh. What did you talk about?'

"I guess I can tell you. He said this was all hush-hush stuff, you know. Don't talk with anybody about the case but I would guess you are the exception."

"I guess so. That's what they always tell you but most doctors I've talked to do it anyway. Especially to their wives."

They were standing next to each other by the lockers that were provided to the surgical medical staff. Frank motioned that they sit in the near- by chairs. Besides, Ken was a bit taller than him and he always felt just a bit awkward looking up, even in the operating suite.

"Well, he covered pretty much the same stuff we both know about. He seemed to know one thing, though."

Frank tried not to look way as he asked him what the lawyer did seem to know.

'He told me it seemed your defense is aimed at putting most of the blame, if there is any, on me."

Frank remained ominously quiet and proceeded to tie his shoe again.

""Really? That's what he told you." Yes, sir" Ken quickly replied

"Do you remember if there was anything unusual about the closing of that case, Ken?." "I don't think so. I closed up the valve and the flaps just like I always do."

"Well, that's all you can say. You did what you usually do. I certainly wouldn't contest that statement."

Frank thought that might sew up this conversation. He wanted it to end. Ken wasn't about to accommodate him.

"OK. How come my lawyer says he heard that was your defense?"

"I'm not sure, Ken, Really" Frank felt a bit of guilt over that. It was a lie, he knew, but it wasn't the time or place to challenge Ken. Hopefully, this whole thing would be all right in the end. That seemed to sooth his conscience a bit. "Look, I'm still thinking that we win this one. There were so many reasons for what happened. It probably had nothing to do with either one of us."

Ken's face screwed up [into a visage of either disbelief or scorn. Frank couldn't discern what.

"I hope you are right, Dr. Martin. But... this thing is bothering the shit out of me,"

"Ken. It's early in your career but I'm sure you know choosing surgery put you into a rather high category on the pyramid of legal risk taking in our present litigious society. This is the first time I have been sued but the older guys keep reassuring me this is part of the' business' if you will and you can't let it eat into your marrow. You always do what you think is the best thing for your patients and if crap happens, it happens."

Frank wished he believed all of this. He was trying to present this Potemkin-like facade of calm amidst the storm. Maybe this was to reassure Ken, maybe to reassure himself, or maybe it was all bullshit.

"Listen, Ken. It might be longer than either of us would like before this thing comes to an actual trial. You and I are going to continue working together and doing what we do best. That's really all we can do at this point."

"I guess I know all of that. But, thanks for the reassurance."

The days stretched into weeks and slowly Frank let his days be filled with other than the thoughts of the trial. He was glad for that. Even Carole told him she had noticed he seemed a bit more relaxed at home both her and the kids. At first, all of this had seem to interfere with their sexual relationship and this bothered him more than her. With this slow passing of time, however, the inhibitory clouds seemed to drift away a bit. It was one of those nights when all went well.

"Frank, that was good, honey."

She told him after they were finished. "Good. I liked it too."

"You seem to be so much more relaxed than you have been lately" "Do you think?"

"I know. Not just think."

"Well, I think I have devised the Frank Martin path to malpractice equanimity." He told her with that sing-song manner that she recognized was playful.

"Oh? And what that might mean?"

Frank looked over at his wife. She was truly beautiful. That radiant face of hers always seemed to send the same warm felling through him. No question about it. She was one of his pillars. He had always felt himself to be a tough guy who could handle everything thrown a him. He still did but having her with him seemed to enrich that feeling of invincibility.

"Well, sweetie. It goes lot this: I did no wrong. That is my song. You cannot find an innocent man guilty. Besides, I always do the best I can and let the pieces fall where they may. Nothing I can do about it now, anyway."

She laughed a quiet laugh.

"Well, Dr. Martin. That certainly sounds as close to Oliver Wendell Holmes s I have ever heard." She quietly clapped her hands together "Good job. Now, sweetie, just believe it!" "Oh I do, I do!" And with that he embraced her once more and to his surprise, was able to perform again. But, deep down he wasn't sure he did. And Ken's face still seemed to be peering at him.

CHAPTER TEN

It was a cool but sunny early Fall day when, after calling his office as he always did at the end of day in surgery, his receptionist told him a Mr. Donnaldson had called and wished for him to contact him as his earliest convenience. Frank was uncertain whether should be anxious or relieved. He leaned back in the chair and looked out the nearby window.

"OK, Frank" he thought "now is the time to get this bullshit on the road. Go call the son of -a-bitch."

He dialed the number he had and Donnaldson's office answered. They put him through to him quicker than he thought they would. Why are lawyers always 'in a meeting'? But not now, I guess.

"Dr. Martin. Yes. Thanks for calling back so soon. Just to let you know that the trial date has been set"

Frank felt an unexpected cold shudder. Wasn't this what he wanted. To get this goddarnn thing over with. But still…

"Yes, When?"

'October 20th. One month from now."

One month? Is that enough time for us… you… to prepare our defense?" There was a pause. Was that an insult, Frank thought.

"Dr, Martin. I've been there and done this before, believe me. I have not been idle. We shall indeed be ready."

"I mean, do you have. Do you need what o they call them, an expert witness?"

"Of course. I have contacted a Dr. Harold Campbell. He is a well respected Cardiovascular surgeon from New York"

"New York? I haven't heard of him and why not someone from Chicago. There are a hell of a lot of them here and I hear it's best to get someone from your own city, if possible."

"Please, Dr. Martin. You take care of the hearts and Ill do the legal stuff, OK"

What the fuck, Frank thought. What kind of a haughty bastard is this? He did get that impression from the first time he had met him but he did come highly recommended.

"Sure. This is the first time this has ever happened to me and to tell you the truth, it is scaring the shit out of me. Worrying too much, aren't I?" "Nonsense. Every doctor who is sued worries. but, remember, most of the time, it is the doctor defendant who wins. So let's approach this in a calm way. By the way, the plaintiff's attorney needs to take your deposition before the actual trial date. How is next Monday for you? I think you told me you don't always operate on Mondays."

It so happened that he wasn't this coming Monday. He knew that already. "Sure... sure. That's fine. What do I do for that one?"

"Nothing. Just show up. But be certain you stick to the facts. They will use you testimony in court. I'll be there with you, obviously, so don't worry. Be here in my office at 9:00. The deposition will be at 10:00"

Frank drove home that day with mixed emotions. The passing scenery, which he always seem to enjoy as a contrast to the hospital, once again seemed a blur. He hadn't had that feeling since this first began. Dinner was more solemn than usual although he did not want his children to sense any despair on his part. He calmly told Carol and them of his call and conversation with Donnaldson "Daddy, you're not going to jail, are you?" Teri asked him with more apprehension than he wanted to hear. Laughing as he answered he told her this was not that kind of trial and no jail time was involved, He told her that in a rather matter-of fact manner and that seemed to satisfy her, And him. Tim didn't ask anything and Frank was uncertain what that meant.

"Son, how was school today?" he asked as he often did at dinner time. "Fine, Dad. Nothing big. Usual stuff, you know." "What are you studying in history?" That was Frank's avocation and he tried to read as much as he could when time allowed, which never seemed to be enough

"The origin of the American Constitution." Tim answered. There followed a interchange between them that seemed to highlight Tim's intelligence which he and Carole both recognized as gifted. But Frank knew that also enabled him to have more insight into what Frank had told them about the upcoming trial. God, this shit is no fun.

Later that a night, when both Tim and Teri were asleep and he and Carole were in the living room looking at but not really seeing what was on he television screen, Carole told him she was glad this was coming to some sort of a conclusion, one way or the other.

"So am I, honey" he told her" it is affecting me more than it should, I know but I just can't seem to help it. My steel armor, you know, seems to be rusting,"

Marvin Thomas

Carole smiled at him but deep down she knew that was true. She had always admired him both for his intelligence and seemingly impenetrable character: strong and decisive "Bullshit." she said. "My strong shining knight remains atop his white horse, battering the windmills with his insouciant sword."

"That was a hell of mouthful" he exclaimed and with that they embraced and drifted into a pleasant night of sex, which he found helpful.

CHAPTER ELEVEN

The deposition could not come too quickly. He had floated through those weeks doing what had to be done. He reminded himself that he was a professional and professional do what they had to do no matter what. He had performed the usual menu of surgical procedures. One or two were quite complex but he and Ken had worked rather well together through all of this. Ken never talked to him again about the case and he really did not know here his resident stood in terms of preparation. He never asked. But he still felt uncomfortable with him but not enough to prevent them from doing what had to be done. They were, after all, professionals.

The deposition was somewhat intriguing. The plaintiff's lawyer, a Mr. Harold Katz, was cordial and smooth. Donnaldson was by his side throughout the proceedings and he did not feel uncomfortable. Katz reviewed the entire case and continued to press him about his and Ken's involvement. Donnaldson kept steering him towards their major defensive thrust: it was not his fault, if there was any, it was the resident, Ken. While this was not specifically spelled out, of course, the inferences were plain to hear. As his testimony continued, Frank became more comfortable with the wall they were trying to construct. A legal recorder was taking this all down so Frank was aware that this could be part of the testimony that was to come. After the deposition, Donnaldson congratulated him on his even temperament and keen answers. "That was quite good, Frank. "It was the first time he had used his first name. "You needed very little help from me. I think our defense looks reasonably solid now"

"Really"

"Well, yes. Are you questioning my judgment?" "Not at all. Just being certain"

"Of course. Trust me, Dr. Martin. Everything I am doing is in your best interest. Please understand that."

Frank had noticed he had switched back to the more formal 'Dr' He wasn't sure what to make of that but perhaps he was reading too much into this legal stuff.

"I do." he answered and they left it at that.

He was a bit more on edge over the next few weeks waiting for the trial date. Donnaldson had told him the length of that trial was indeterminate but he advised him that he should be in the courtroom for the entire proceedings. The jury always looked more kindly upon that. He advised him to mark out at least two, maybe, three weeks from his schedule. He also told him that the date of that trial can change.

"What do you mean, change?" Frank asked incredulously.

"Just that. It happens. More often than I like."

"That's a bit disturbing to say the least. What kind of bullshit is that? I mean, what do I do, just quit doing surgery for the next few months or what?"

Donnaldson looked at him with that peculiar expression that would become all too familiar. Frank would also learn that in spite of his somewhat patrician demeanor he was actually a very good lawyer. "Yes, it is a bit shitty isn't it? But, hopefully it will begin as scheduled. No, just block our three weeks. That should do it." "That was also the first time that Frank had heard him use anything but proper English. It would not be the last.

"Thanks. So, what now. Just wait until the day it is supposed to begin?'

"More or less. Do not, and I repeat, do not discuss any of this with your colleagues. Particularly Dr. Laser."

"Fine. I have told my wife."

"Expected. That's all right. Now, as hard as this may be, just go about your way until that trial begins. Cancel that time. I have some more work to do but you don't, as far as this is concerned. I'll be in contact before then and discuss more of this with you.

Good luck, Frank. I think we will be fine. And, please call me Alan."

"Sure enough." Frank shook his hand and felt more at ease about all of this. He even had forgotten about Ken Laser for awhile. But he thought of him again now.

CHAPTER TWELVE

Frank had cancelled three weeks of his surgery schedule. It was difficult, seeing that some of the cases were somewhat urgent. Two patients elected to go with another surgeon whom he had recommended. One was quite challenging and he hated to pass up the opportunity to use all of his skills but *c 'est la vie* he thought. Donnaldson had called him two nights before the trial date.

"Frank. The date is set. No postponements."

'Glad to hear that" he answered with a tone of relief.

"Frank. Wear a suit to the courtroom every day. That always impresses a jury. And, if at all possible, bring your wife to sit by your side. That shows what a solid family man you are."

"Really?"

"Yes. Listen Frank, This is about drama as much as about science and facts. Unfortunately. But that is the way it is. Don't fight it. I will see you there at 8:30. The jury selection will be starting at 9:00. I assume you know where the courthouse is located."

"Yes"

"Good. See you then. Any questions?" "No. Not really."

When he hung up, he thought about what he had just heard. This is about theater as much as it is about the facts.

He probably knew that but what a ton of bull shit. Two professional lives are in balance and two actors will be on stage to help decide that. What bullshit But, yes, that's the way it is. I want to fight it I really do but I cannot. He knew he had to resign himself to what the system was and try not to fight it. It would be hard. This is not the way he was used to thinking. Logic may not be the principal factor. But Jesus, they have to listen to the facts. They just have to.

He had wrapped things up in his office and told his secretary to 'hold the fort' until all of this was over. Cynthia was a middle-aged woman in her early fifties, married, with two boys. One in high school yet, the other in his second year of college. She as pleasant and very efficient. Not terribly attractive, she compensated with her sparkling approach to life and people. He treasured her. And she admired him.

"God, Dr. Martin. You know I'll be thinking of you. This stuff must really make you angry."

"Cynthia, you don't know the half of it. It genuinely pisses me off"

She blushed at the use of that mild profanity but she was no 'prude'.

"I bet. You know I wish you the best of luck. Keep me up to date please. I'll hold the fort down, don't worry about that. Just go and give them hell. You'll do just fine."

"I appreciate your vote of confidence. And knowing you are here helps. It really does. I'll call you every day. But, if there is anything, anything, I really need to answer, call my wife's cell. I think she'll be with me in the courtroom"

He had talked to Carole about that and she was more than eager to be with him. That helped. He had sat and talked to both of his children and explained what the next few weeks might be like. Surprisingly, they seemed to understand in that childish way that satisfies everyone.

The morning of the trial came up crisp but sunny. Frank slept better than he thought he would and while he considered sex that night, both he and Carole seemed to ease away from it. Probably better, he thought. Save it for some other time. He picked out a nice but conservative blue suit and a reasonable tie to accent it. Carole approved of both. She wore a moderately seductive outfit that dampened her attractive figure but highlighted her beauty otherwise. Good to impress the male jurors, perhaps, he thought. Theater, you know.

"Well, honey. Finally. Let's get this over with" she told him "Amen. I need to get my life back in order." "I think you've handled yourself quite well"

"Do you? Well, maybe I've looked like the beacon of calm but inside I have been churning. Really churning"

"I know, Frank. I could tell you were putting on a bit of a charade but still, you,... well... you were calmer than than most, I would think."

With that, they left the house and took the drive to the courthouse. It was a stately edifice. The marble seemed to engulf them. Frank would never forget that feeling. It would always remind him of what a courthouse should look like. The majesty of the law and all that.

Donnaldson was standing in the hallway so he would know which room they were to enter. It was the first time Carole had met him. While Frank had told her that he was the 'personification of a lawyer' she was taken aback by his stately features and elegant manner of dress.

"Good morning, Frank. I see you had no trouble maneuvering through the Chicago traffic and finding your way here. And I presume this beautiful lady is your wife?."

"Carole, this is Mr. Alan Donnaldson"

"So good to meet you, Mrs. Martin. You will add a glamorous touch to these rather dull proceedings that will soon commence."

Thank you" Carole quietly replied. She wasn't sure if this patrician style he was projecting was all bluff or the real thing. But she suspected either way it must impress anyone in a courtroom. "Frank has told me so much about you. We both feel we are in good hands."

"Well I do hope so and I am confident he is… Now, the first part of this will be the jury selection. While you are not directly involved in this, of course, I would welcome any suggestions or thoughts you have about any of the prospective jurors. Since this is a civil and not criminal case, this doesn't usually take that much time. However, it still is just as important in a very different way, of course."

He led them in to the courtroom. It was a bit smaller than Frank imagined it would be but otherwise looked just like those he had seen countless times on television and in movies. But now it was more personal. The floors were polished tile and in the sunlight they glistened like mirrors. Wooden panels encased the remainder of the room. In front on a minimally elevated dais was the judge's desk. It was larger than Frank thought it needed to be but he suspected that served some sort of judicial purpose. Not far from that was, obviously, the jury box. It was empty now. He led them to a smaller desk across from the judge

Marvin Thomas

that was the defense attorney's area. Besides his there were chairs for Ken Laser and his attorneys. That remark ignited another surge of that emotion which continued to plague Frank, but he let it pass. Across from them was another row of tables that were for the plaintiffs. Frank and Carole had arrived before anyone else. Behind all of that were about a eight rows of seats for the general public should anyone wish to sit in. Donnaldson told Carole she should sit directly behind her husband.

Not long after, Ken walked into the room, his tall figure accentuated by the relative diminutive stature of his attorney. Donnaldson recognized him immediately and went over to shake his hand.

"Sam how nice to see you again." While the two of them had talked about the case, since Frank and Ken were co-defendants, they apparently had not personally met but obviously were familiar with each other.

"Same here, Alan. Haven't really seen you in months, for some reason. How's Lillian?"

Frank assumed he was referring to his wife but maybe not. At any rate, the answer was not confirmatory of either.

"Good, good. Sam. Thanks for asking. And Martha?"

"Doing well. We must get together soon, Alan, missed going out with you two."

"Certainly. Just give us a ring anytime. Good luck on this."

"Obviously, you too."

As Donnadlson walked back, Frank studied the other attorney. He was short, a bit pudgy, and without the patrician look of Donnaldson. His hair was a bit unkempt and his clothes seemed to not fit well.

"That is Sam Kopsberg. You'd never know he was a Harvard graduate, would you? But he is really quite brilliant like they all seem to be. Probably could have stayed on there and who knows, become/me a high-falutin judge. But, his family is here in Chicago and his wife wanted to return. He is with one of the other prestigious firms in the city. Damn good man."

Frank took the 'like they all seem to be' comment to be a mild ethnic slur against his Jewish background but at the same time Donnaldson seemed to think highly of him so he couldn't really tell if there was any true anti Semitism here.

Frank was uncertain if he should go and talk with Ken. He elected, instead, to simply acknowledge his presence. Ken nodded his head. Didn't seem too upset, Frank thought. He stiffened a bit as he saw Mr and Mrs. Johnson enter the room. He had not seen her in several months. Jesus Christ! She is still in a wheelchair! What the fuck is this? He thought. He had thought she at least would be walking with assistance. Was this some sort of a act? He remembered Donnaldson's admonition that the courtroom was more theater than law. Sitting down next to them was a tall, young man with glasses that seemed to large for his face.

"That is George Clark "Donnaldson said." He's a tough son-of -a bitch. Good though. Went to a state school." He said that with emphasis as if that put him on a lower level than him or Kopsberg. So now the legal teams were complete. If Frank wasn't so intimately involved he thought this might be a match worth watching. To complete the scene before the jury selection, the presiding judge walked in and all stood. The judge was a middle-aged rather rotund man with graying hair and a thin, drawn face that magnified his basic homeliness. Frank thought he was out of place in this scene.

"Who is the judge, Alan?"

"That is the venerable George Timms. Ugly bastard isn't he? "Frank was surprised and amazed at that remark. But he was dead on. "Honest guy. Even-handed. But to everyone. In sum, a good guy to have on the case."

Frank assumed that was good news and he tried to assimilate that into his perception of the courtroom as theatre. Guess that works, he decided.

The next step he was told by Donnaldson was the most important. The choosing of the jury.

"In this theater, the actors are on the stage. The jurors are the audience. But all of them are the critics. So each will have a voice in how they view the acting and if they give thumbs up to one side or the other."

"So, one again, facts don't play a big role here."

"Frank, my man. Don't get me completely wrong. The acting is the thing but the facts are the ceiling against which the acting will stop. Make sense?"

Frank thought about what he had just said. Somehow, he found that comforting.

"Yea, I guess. I do admit I find that reassuring. I think."

CHAPTER THIRTEEN

Years later, Frank could still remember every one of the twelve who were ultimately chosen for that jury. It was, in fact, the extension of the process Donnaldson had described. There had been an agreement between Donnadlson and Kopsberrg that Donnaldson should be the lead attorney for the defense. Frank was uncertain how this was determined but that was between those two. Both he and Clark approached the selection process in a minuet, whirling about as in a chess game

"There is an art in jury selection, Frank" he had told him. "An important art. I will try, as the defense attorney, to determine, the best I can, if there seems to be any hostility towards physicians, particularly surgeons. Difficult to do but necessary. I will also try to select those who seem bright enough to understand some medical jargon but, as I said, that's a smaller part of this whole equation."

The first two potential jurors were dismissed for reasons not entirely clear to Frank. The third, a bespectacled middle-aged man was, surprisingly, a biology teacher at a local junior high. He was selected immediately. The second, a attractive young woman, not much older than 30,

Frank thought, was a secretary for a distribution center,. Unmarried, apparently, by the absence if a wedding band, propelled Donnalson to chose her on the primary basis that Frank was a quite handsome man and that would draw some attention and perhaps sympathy. That, thought Frank, is a bit ridiculous but what the hell. He's the boss… Kopsberg challenged the next juror and since there was no dissent they went on to choose the third and fourth who, while both blue collar workers, were middle aged and had no obvious disqualifications. The fifth chosen struck Frank as intriguing. He was the president of small regional bank on the far north side of Chicago. Well dressed, he had an air of some one who wanted be here as if he was carrying the torch of justice for society. Why Donnaldson did not challenge him was a mystery but apparently he could not challenge that many and had reassured Frank that he was as likely to rule for him as against him. The sixth was an older woman in her 60's who was a retired nurse. Frank felt the most comfortable with that. Finally someone who might be able to ascend above the theatrics here. But she had this hardened look about her that bothered him. Did she feel that she had not been appreciated by some or all the doctors in her past life? Did she feel that these malpractice suits often got out of hand? Next was an older man, balding but with that sort of pleasant smile that is often bewildering in terms of what the person is really thinking. He was a welder of Italian descent. No surprises here and he was seated as the seventh juror. The eighth and ninth picks were both females. The first was in her seventies, Frank surmised, worked as a secretary and had retired ten years before. She had the typical visage of a woman who had not been very attractive when young and now was assuming the role of the matron of something.

Next came a younger woman Frank guessed was around fifty. She was a housewife with two sons in college. Her husband had died two years earlier and she was struggling a bit to make ends meet but her employer who seemed very supportive and did not hesitate to back her for jury duty. The tenth juror, a tall fairly rugged -looking man no older than thirty told them he was an accountant in one of the large Chicago firms. He had been there since graduating from the University of Illinois. Frank had the impression that he was quite bright but was so quiet you could hardly understand him. However, neither side had any objections. Next to be chosen was a black man who worked as a janitor in a large office building. But he had always wanted to be on a jury and seemed eager to be able to do so for this trial. Frank wondered how he would fit in with the rest but stopped himself from going further, 'don't be racist' he told himself. Finally came another young woman. Maybe in her early forties, who was a commercial artist now working for a company that published medical materials. Now, Frank thought, here is someone who also can understand what this is all about. But why should someone who just drew renditions of parts of the body know more than the janitor about what had happened? Silly for him to think she necessarily would. But she was seated and that completed the jury selection.

"Well, the most interesting part of this whole process is over. Frank, what do you think of our lineup? Maybe too may blue collar types you know. They kinda like the little guy. But, I couldn't keep all of them off.
"I guess it's OK" But his remarks about blue collar types bothered him a bit. Class warfare here ?

"Yes. I should think so. I am, in general; pleased." Now, let the games begin" he said with a firmness. "And remember. Like I told you before :Do not be arrogant. Come across as a humble, honest doctor trying to do his best with all his patients. Got that?" "Yes." Frank resented his condescension but knew was the pro here so I'll be a piece of humble pie.

The 'games', as he described them, rolled along in front of him like he was watching something on a movie screen. While he was not always in that screen he and Ken seemed to be the main actors. While had ran the events of that day through his mind many times this was as if someone was retelling the story to him from a distance. His anxiety would float like a wave rising to the surface whenever the word 'mistake,. unfortunate, neurological deficits, and disability 'appeared on the screen. He canvassed each of the jurors more than he wished. These were, he decided, the audience also observing the drama being played out. But a sinking feeling he had told him that this was a special audience whose judgment would carry more consequences than anyone he had ever sat next to in a movie theater. For one of the few times in his life, he was experiencing that displeasing feeling of insecurity.

Donnaldson and Kopsberg seemed to be an effective tandem. That Kopsberg impressed Frank. He was as smooth a talker as he had ever heard. And could use words like tools::building each one into a structure that seemed to suit each moment. Impressive. No wonder Donnaldson had such high regards for him. Donnaldson wasn't bad himself. Or so he thought. George Clark, on the other hand, seemed to be the sort of person you would have guessed was from the Mid-west. The twang of that distinctive Chicago accent highlighted his speech in a easily identified fashion. He chose words that seemed not framed in ancient Greek or Latin. which Donnaldson and Kopsberg used to project that aura of Ivy League East Coast patina, Frank wasn't sure how effective that was going to be in a setting like this. Clark seemed to recognize the level of sophistication of that special audience more clearly. Strange. Both of the defense attorneys were experienced and would be expected to gear their presentation on a more homey level, particularly with the technical medical jargon that was involved even with Kopsberg's magnificent command of the English language. But maybe he was being a bit too concerned and judgmental. Objectivity was not his strong suit these days. He listened intently as the case was laid out. It came down to whether there had been negligence on the part of him or Ken or both. He tried to focus on that group of twelve across from him. As Donnaldson had said, these were the critics and they would judge how the play went. Some seemed to pay vivid attention, others not. How interested were they really? Was this something they wanted to do or just had to do?

Frank still felt as if he was in a dream as the day proceeded. When they broke for lunch, there was a choice to eat in the court cafeteria or find another venue Donnaldson suggested they go out of the building.

"It's bit crowed in the cafeteria. Besides, we don't want to run into anyone else, if you know what I mean" he told them.

Frank didn't quite know what he did mean except he wasn't sure he wanted to see Ken just yet. The case was edging a bit towards their agreed strategy. Something may have happened but if so, it was primarily Ken's negligence, not his.

"Sure. You know the area, pick a spot" he told him. Carole agreed.

Walking out of the building into a crisp sunny day was like a breath of fresh air indeed. He was grateful for the choice to leave Still a dream but a more pleasant one now. They walked a few blocks west to a small but cheerful lunch spot. There were outside tables and they chose to sit in the one that was empty. Carole seemed to be even more beautiful with the sun reflecting off her smooth face. He wondered if her appearance really influenced any of those jurists. Maybe. That thought struck him as bit odd. His and Ken's career on the line in part based on the beauty or lack thereof of his wife or any other person. Strange. He ordered his favorite, a tuna melt, along with a glass of white wine. Carole, adding to her usual salad, a glass of iced tea.

"Ah, I see the lady goes the salad route." Donnaldson quipped. "So does my wife. Even got me into the swing. Health thing she says. Do you agree, doctor?" he asked: "You know the old saying, a man's wife knows more about how he should eat than the man", Frank answered.

"Really? Never heard that one. Is that in some of your medical texts?" "No. I think I saw it in a law book. Chapter was 'Spousal Law. 101"

The three of them visibly laughed at that one and it certainl y relaxed Frank and Carole. "Touche, Dr. Thompson. Well, what do you think of the first day?"

"I really can't say. I'm watching the jury as well as Ken and Mrs. Johnson Don't you guys have to call in some sort of 'expert witness'?"

"Oh, I thought I had talked with you about that already."
"No"

Dannaldson gave him that smug half-smile that Frank had become accustomed to. "Well, we have retained the services of Doctor Robert Kelly. Used him once or twice. Excellent man."

"Never heard of him"

"I said he is retired. Probably several years older than you"

"I thought you would ask me my opinion on any expert witness"

"We usually do but I have so much confidence in Lincoln that I didn't think that would be necessary"

"Jesus, Alan, what kind of shit is that?"

"Frank!" Carole exclaimed through the salad she had not yet chewed.

"Really Doctor. No reason to jump on me. He is good. I guarantee you. I am truly sorry if our choice offends you."

"Not that, really I guess" Frank limply replied. "But I thought that was the custom." "It won't happen again" Donnaldson told him in an obvious attempt to exit this part of the conversation.

"Well, let's hope there is no again." Carole interjected also hoping to move on. The three of them continued to eat their lunch in relative silence for the next several minutes, trying to let a wave of quiet time sooth the atmosphere.

"And you, Mrs Martin. What are your impressions of the first day thus far?"

Carole continued to eat for a few seconds trying to mobilize her thoughts in a cogent whole.

"You and Mr. Kopsberg were impressive" "Thank you. And?"

"I don't know what else to say. I guess it went all right. I have been watching the jury too. I have made some eye contact with some of them."

"The men, I presume"

"What does that mean?" she asked somewhat angrily.

"It means nothing, my dear. Beauty has a way of seeping into these drab courtroom surroundings and lighting up the place, if you will."

"Thanks, I guess" Carole answered. "But I am still am not sure what you are saying." "Nothing important. But, those eyes are helpful"

Carole decided to leave the subject at that. But she knew what he meant. OK, she thought, if that helps Frank I'll give them all the eye they want. Dannaldson then turned to Frank.

"You may be called to the stand d this afternoon. Might not be until tomorrow or the next day. But I do want to reiterate that you should not act as if this whole thing pisssses you off and it is an imposition on your time and an affront to your good name and that it is even happening. Too may of my physician clients give that impression on the stand and it is suicide, believe me."

I think you told me that before." Frank retorted "I understand. I'll try my best to keep an even keel." "Good"

They finished the meal talking about a few other unrelated matters and Dannaldson asked for the check.

"Let's take a small stroll before we go back into the courtroom. It'll help clear our minds."

Frank was thankful for that. The warm, Fall sun did sooth him. Carole seemed to look even more beautiful under it. Frank couldn't help but notice Dannaldson giving her a few more looks than he thought was necessary. But oh well. She is beautiful if I say so myself. He was a little disappointed that they had to end their short walk and enter back into the marble mausoleum but the play was about to resume.

CHAPTER FOURTEEN

Nothing really had changed. The twelve critics were back in their seats and the actors in their assigned places, ready for the next act to begin It was time for George Clark to present the other side. Carole smiled at Frank as the proceedings began. George Clark was everything that Donnaldson had said. Plain spoken, humble in his manner and speaking that characteristic twang of Chicago. He traced the story of Harriet Johnson from the day she was sent to Frank's office through the surgery and its aftermath. Frank sank into his chair as he listened. Clark was not hostile nor demonstrative but deliberate in his construction of the tale. Woven into it was the suspicion that Frank and Ken were incompetent in this one instance. Not always but then. And that incompetence had led to the tragedy that was now Harriet Johnson. A once vibrant woman, smart and beautiful who was so extraordinarily active Clark was deliberate as he pointed her out to the jury. In that wheelchair even Frank felt a horrific twang of guilt. Was he, in fact, responsible for what he saw. He glanced across the room at Ken Laser. Such innocence. The visage of youth, carved with all the implications of a long future still ahead. Now, facing this test of adversity. Did he really screw things up. He swears he didn't but did he? How many of his colleagues had told him, over and over it seemed, that this suing 'shit' was just 'part of doing business'. God, that was crap. It took you over the emotional coals. It gnawed at you like a constant saw with a fucking black cloud of doubt never quite out of the picture. What was this doing to him? He was such a good kid and really, a damn good young surgeon. But, it was not my fault. It just wasn't my fault.

Clark next proceeded to have Harriet Johnson take the stand or to take the oath in her wheel chair. She was a strikingly beautiful woman, even Frank had to admit.
Not quite as beautiful as before the surgery but still very attractive. She had great difficulty talking, slurring her words such that it sounded like a engine out of whack. Perhaps she could do better than this but she was very effective in projecting the picture of a once vibrant woman reduced to what the critics now were seeing.

Donnaldson leaned over to him.
"Very effective, Frank, Very effective. That sort of stuff is a real killer for us, believe me. But, remember our defense is that we had nothing to so with this. Our defense sits across the room" he nodded in the direction of Ken Laser.
Frank nodded back but did not quiet the lingering sense of total unease. After all he was the head surgeon, literally responsible for whatever occurred in that operating room. But still, he was too good of a surgeon to have this happen so maybe all of it was Ken's fault. He listened with riveting attention to Harriet. Out came the story, again, of her visit to Frank on that, what was now, a fateful day in his office and the decision to go ahead with valve repair. The tale was slowly spun out. How she had awakened unable to move

and speak well. The absolute horror of it all! And the horror continued. She was almost helpless. Her husband had to do so much for her. She was able to paint that picture of how this has cut her active life down to... what they all saw now. Frank wondered when and who Clark would use as his expert witness. Did he have one? Did he think he might not even need one? Was the sight and sounds of Harriett Johnson simply enough? Those questions were answered soon enough.

Your honor" Clark intoned as he turned to Judge Wilson "I'd like to bring into this courtroom Dr. Robert Kelly. Dr Kell y is one of the most eminent cardiac surgeons in the country."

"Yes, of course Mr. Clark. But I don't think you need any adjectives at this point." "Yes, of course, Sorry your honor. Please have the clerk strike that remark from the record." Of course, Frank knew the point had been made.

Frank watched as a tall, rather plain looking man with glasses that seemed too large for his thin face stood up and walked to the stand. He had a vague recollection of this Dr. Kelly. When Clark did the introductions and informed all he was from New York it did ring a bell. Robert Kelly. Of course. He had attended a refresher when he was still at Harvard. Seemed like a nice guy then. And rather knowledgeable. Good pick, Clark, Frank thought. Kelly took the stand, going through the swearing-in routine and rattled off his credentials as directed. He spoke with a deeper voice than expected given the body habitus. Confidence oozed from his every pore. Sort of like me, Frank thought. "Now, Dr. Kelly," Clark started his interrogation "have you ever performed a similar procedure as Mrs. Johnson endured?'

Marvin Thomas

"Of course" he answered swiftly "This is not uncommon surgery.:"

"And, have you ever had a similar outcome.?" "No,. not a similar one as this."

"I see. Can you tell the jury, in your own words, s to what you think did occur during that procedure that resulted in the condition we are all viewing at this time?"

Donnaldson immediately objected saying that question would lead only to speculation. He was, as Frank expected, overruled as the judge felt that the testimony was indeed pertinent to this case.

Kelly proceeded to describe all the possible reasons for this outcome. He went t into more detail as Clark pushed him towards the conclusion that it was most likely a human error on the part of one or both surgeons.

"Yes, of course. That is the most likely scenario but not the only one, of course, only the most likely in this case."

His testimony ran into almost a half hour. Clark thanked him when he was finished. It was now the defense attorney's time.

Kopsberg went first. His sauntering approach to the witness stand highlighted the man's deliberate style.

"Good afternoon, Dr. Kelly:" he began "always a pleasure to meet and interview such a distinguished person." Frank wondered why he used such a gratuitous approach

"Now, you say you have never had an outcome such as the one we have been hearing about in this situation. That seems hard to believe. How many of these procedures have you indeed performed?".

"I do not, of course, have an exact number, but perhaps close to one hundred."

Frank thought that was plausible. Kelly looked to be in his mid-sixties, certainly enough time to do that many. And he was at an important referral center in a respected academic setting.

After exploring a bit, Kopsberg struck home with a question that actually startled Frank. "What do you think went wrong here, doctor?'

Kelly sat still for a moment or two. Maybe he wasn't expecting such a penetrating question.'

"I cannot say with certainty, of course. But upon reviewing the proceedings very carefully over the past month or so, it appears that something happened a the tail end of the surgery that wasn't supposed to happen that led to either an embolus to her brain or a leak of blood that caused enough hypotension, that is, low blood pressure, to compromise her brain"

"Was that the result of a surgical miscue or, perhaps, the anesthesiologist missing a cue?"

"It could have been either or both"

With that he told Kopsberg that he had no further questions.

"Mr. Donnaldson, do you wish to cross-examine"

Frank surmised they had discussed the order in which they would do the cross-exam as Donnaldson stood up and answered he did and strode to the witness box with that solid air of authority that he seemed to project. His appearance seemed to make an impression on the jury that Carole noticed. almost immediately. Kelly eyed him keenly and nodded when he introduced himself. He went through his resume briefly and then began to question him.

"Doctor, you stated that this unfortunate outcome might have been due to either a miscue on the part of one of the surgeons or the anesthesiologist. Is that correct?" "Yes, that is what I said."

"In your opinion, if there was a human miscue, might that have taken place towards the end of the surgery?"

"I don't know if you can pinpoint a certain time"

"Well, no, but, in your opinion, might that have been more likely towards the end of the procedure?"

"Yes, I would say more likely towards the end."

"And, could it also be possible that this was serendipity, simply an accident of nature without a human cause that can be discerned?:"

"Yes, it is possible but…" "But, what, Doctor?" "Less likely" Donnaldson thought there might be an objection from Clark on that but Kelly's last answer seemed to caused him to refrain.

Donnaldson continued to press his point that if this was a human error it was probably more likely to have occurred towards the end of the procedure. Kelly co-operated in the affirmative and Frank sensed just what was happening. Donnaldson was indeed pushing towards the defense that would be the ultimate fall-back: if there was a human error it would not be Frank's but Ken's. That cloud of guilt momentarily floated again but was gone in a whisper. He looked over at Ken. Unexpectedly, Ken's eyes met his and there seemed to be a sense of surrender in them. Does he know where we are heading? Frank thought. Maybe. Kopsberg is a smart guy. I'm sure he might have anticipated some of this. But if there had been an error, it was surely Ken's fault and not mine. The rerun of that had seared his brain so often that he now was quite certain that this indeed was the truth. The truth, by God.

When Donnaldson had ended his cross-examination, it was indeed Kopsberg time. A last minute whisper to Ken preceded his slow but deliberate saunter to the witness stand. His questioning was exact and incisive. As he proceeded, Donnaldson leaned over to Frank. "I think I know where he is going with this."

"Where"

"It was nobody's fault. It was an act of God if you will. Unavoidable and… improvable." Frank, of course, knew this was what Ken's defense would be. What else was there? "Yeah, that makes sense" he answered after a moment of hesitation to signal maybe, he really didn't know.

He listened more intently now as Kopsberg continued his re- examination. He tried without success to avoid looking across the room from time to time at Ken. What will this do to him if we lose this case. Jesus, such a nice kid. Such a story getting to where he is now./ But, for now, for now.

"So, Dr. Kelly" Kopsberg addressed him for the final time. "it is possible, perhaps likely, that the events that occurred during the surgical procedure of Mrs. Johnson was no one person's fault? It was an unfortunate event that could not have been prevented?"

Again, Kelly hesitated. He looked at Kopsberg studying the intent of that question. Finally, he answered

"It is possible but unlikely."

"Thank you, Dr. Kelly. No more questions, your honor"

So it was now my turn, Frank thought. What did Donnaldson say? The critics are watching each person as if an actor in the ongoing drama. Play the role right and you'll have them eating out of your hand. What a fucking strange justice system, but, oh well.

And it was his turn to testify. Donnaldson had urged him to look sincere and not be argumentative. Let the critics see you as a thoughtful and compassionate surgeon who was a victim of circumstances bu not the perpetrator of any 'mistake' He turned around and smiled at Carole who warmly returned her own in a silent gesture of both pride and reassurance.

As Frank strode confidently to the witness stand he could not help but notice the gazes of the women on the jury. Hell yes, he thought, use the sex appeal stuff to your advantage in this movie.

After being sworn in, he was first questioned by Donnaldson. who constructed his questioning in a manner that was obviously designed to project Frank's humanity and caring attitude as well as ease him into the next round of questioning. He had maneuvered the questioning expertly to the point where Frank had to address the issue of Ken Laser and his role in all of this.

"So, Dr. Martin, when you were done with your part of the surgery and ready to have your resident close you felt that all was well?"
"Yes"
"No problems"
"Not that I was made aware of'
"Did you supervise Dr. Laser's completion of the procedure?"
"Not totally, no. It is standard operating procedure to check all of the other matters while the assistant finishes the surgery. Standard stuff."
"Did you have any reason to suspect that anything was wrong with the way Dr. Laser completed the procedure?"
"No. None at all at the time." "At the time?"
"Yes, at the time when we completed the surgery." "Well. Have you had any doubts since.?"

"About what?"

"Dr Laser's technique in this particular situation."

This was the moment of truth and Frank knew it. This was his defense, right or wrong. There was no turning back.

"Well, some."

"Some? What does that mean?"

"If the problem is the suturing, it might have been something that went wrong. But, I think he did all that was asked of him. I truly believe this was an act of God if you will, an act of nature, the way things sometimes go in any surgical procedure."

"I see."

With that, he told the judge he had no further questions. Now, it apparently was Kopsberg's turn.

He was a short man, this Kopsberg. As nattily dressed as anyone Frank had encountered. He had already impressed him and because of that, he was a bit uneasy about what was to come. He knew the attack would be to exonerate Ken or at least pair him with Frank if there was any blame to be laid. But Donnaldson and he had decided on his defense and he would stick with it.

Kopsberg went through the rituals of the cross-examination before getting to the meat of the matter.

"Well, Dr. Thompson, have I sketched an accurate portrayal of what transpired on that day so far?"

"Yes, I think so."

"You think. Did I miss anything?"

"No. It was as accurate as you could have been"

"Thank you. Now, Mr. Clark pointed out the possibility that this could have been something that went astray towards the end of the procedure. Do you agree?" "Yes"

"'What might that have been?"

"I cannot be certain. There might have been a little problem with the final sutures that ultimately leaked or helped form a clot. I really don't know."

"The neurologist at his deposition felt it was an embolus from the heart>" "I know"

"You know that was what happened or that was what the neurologist stated?

"What he stated"

"Who does the final suturing?"

"Depends. If I have an experienced resident with me, I usually let him do it." "Always or usually?"

"Usually"

"And in this case?"

"I believe I let Dr. Laser finish the suturing>" "You believe or do you know?"

Frank knew Ken had finished this case. He had been through the whole damn procedure a hundred or so times since this all began and he was dead certain. But, was this just part of his determination to wrap the cloak of some invincibility around him.? Did he really know for sure that it wasn't him,? Yes he knew.

"I know"

"And do you feel he did everything he was asked to do correctly?" "I have no reason to believe that he did not?"

"None?"

"None."

There. I said it. Yes, I know that I was not at fault. I don't think Ken was but he might have been. I will leave it at that

And that was the end of his cross exam by Kopsberg. He told that to the judge who after some more legal chatting told Frank he could leave the stand. He gave one last glance a at Ken. Ken's eyes seemed to say that he knew I did my best to defend both of them or did they? He just wasn't sure. But he had said what he wanted to say and that was that. It was not his fault. It just wasn't his fault.

It was now Ken's turn. Tall and lanky and usually self-assured, he walked to the witness stand with the look of a defeated man. God, didn't he know this stuff happens every day? Frank thought. Sure, big man, look how this has affected you! It's like they are filleting you to see what makes you tick It eats at your ego and destroys your self-confidence.

They swore Ken in and began the series of interrogations. Ken seemed to be melting a bit under this fire. That surprised Frank. He thought he was a bit tougher than that. When George Clark sauntered up to him, Frank swore he saw perspiration on Ken's forehead. Nothing shocking but his voice was trembling when he started to answer the questions put to him.

"Now, Dr. Laser, I think we've come to the part of the procedure that you were most involved with... the closing as you call it in surgery? "Yes, sir" Ken sheepishly answered. "Through all of the preceding testimony there seems to be a possibility that something went wrong at this closing. Is that your feeling?"

"No sir."

"No?" "No"

Ken was quite emphatic in his answer. Of course that went along with his end of the defense. This was an Act of God, if you will, it was no one's fault. If a mistake had been made, either Ken did not remember it or he wasn't going to admit it, obviously. Frank, in contrast, while also pointing out the probability of an unavoidable complication also had obliquely pointed towards the alternative, it was Ken's mistake and not his. Clark continue to point on the late stages of the surgery and the expert opinion that it was likely that was where the avoidable mistake was made and this was not an Act of God.

Donnaldson leaned over to Frank and whispered that "Clark is a persistent ass isn't he?
It looks like he is getting to Dr. Laser"
Frank nodded in assent. Yes, Ken was getting fizzled. "When he is finished we'll bring in our expert witness."
"Now?" Frank asked in astonishment.
Frank and Ken along with both Kopsberg and Donnaldson had agreed to Mark Turner in place of Dr Kelly. He was a leading cardiac surgeon at Northwestern who Frank knew well and had worked with on occasion. The new strategy was to use a local authority rather than bring someone in from out of state. Donnaldson agreed that the critics were more impressed with local talent. While Ken thought it might be best to use someone, say from an Ivy League institution, he had been overruled by the two attorneys and Frank had no strong preference about that.
Mark Turner was a man in his mid-fifties. Well known in Chicago, he had agreed to be the new expert witness after studying the case report. While he felt it was possible something had gone wrong technically towards the end of the procedure it was just too uncertain and that it was just a likely unavoidable and a unfortunate complication with no fault of anyone. When Judge Wilson asked if there

were any more witnesses, Donnaldson had stood and stated there was and went on to set the introduction for Turner.

He walked to the witness stand with a gait that projected self-confidence. Tall, handsome w with graying hair at the temples, he seemed to radiate the appearance of authority. Frank had always felt comfortable with him and more often than not, intellectually challenged.

Kopsberg was the first to question him. His approach was, as Frank knew it would be, that no one was at fault. Turner did not hesitate in coming to that conclusion. Frank noticed the faces of the critics seemingly impressed with both his appearance, demeanor, and answers. If there was an academy award here, Mark Turner would win hands down. His testimony was so terse and capable that even Frank was now almost convinced that it indeed was simply the fates that had gotten Harriet Johnson.

When Kopsberg had completed his examination, it was Donnaldson's tum. Alan also seemed caught in the magnetism of Mark Turner. Frank had no idea that he would be this good as a witness. Now it was time to not only reaffirm that no one was probably at fault but if so, it was not his client. How would Donnaldson do this without destroying the texture of what had been extracted by Kopsberg?

Frank still could not believe he was here in this room. He still could not keep that musty odor that penetrated every part of him out of his mind. The high ceilings, the arcane look to the architecture, the alienation it seemed to convey, away from the daily rhythms of life that dealt with the very fiber of a person's being. Strange place this. But it was the reality of the moment and he continued to move along as the cameras rolled. From time to time, he looked back at Carol in the row behind him. The smiling face that always greeted him continued to be a anchor. Her beauty never so evident, never so reassuring. But, now, he watched with wariness as Donnaldson began his exam of Mark Turner.

"Good afternoon, Dr Turner. You are aware, of course, of the nature of the charge against Dr. Martin?"

"Yes, sir. I am."

And do you have an opinion about its implication of negligence?" "Yes sir, I do"

"Well, please tell the members of the jury and the judge what that opinion might be." Mark went into rather great detail about the nature of the procedure. He felt the surgery was performed 'according to the book' and that. as he had told Kopsberg, it was an unexpected complication that was probably unavoidable. But Donnaldson wasn't satisfied with that conclusion.

"And, let' say that it was as you outlined it, an unfortunate complication for the lovely Mts. Johnson. But, if an error had been made, and it seems unlikely as you have described it, would it not have been at the conclusion of the procedure itself.?" "Probably" Turner promptly responded. Donnaldson waited for a short time to let that answer marinate with the critics. "Probably or likely?"

"As I said, sir. I feel this was an unfortunate complication of the procedure that did not involve any human error. But probably is my answer to your specific question and there is no way that any of us can be sure."

"Of course not, Doctor, of course not. And, we agree that this was a unfortunate unforeseen adverse event that occurred without any human prompting but Dr. Martin is an impeccable surgeon and wishes for the outcome of these proceedings to reflect that." Donnadslon went on with a few more questions to establish the outstanding character of Frank and touched on Ken in such a peripheral way that it would be hard to tease out his strategy of pointing the finger to him if there was any question still of fault. That, of course, was the his attack plan all along. It still pained Frank and he stole a quick glance at Ken who still seemed shocked by all of this.

Now it was George Clark one on one with Mark Turner. Frank studied Clark's face. He thought he noticed a grin that was either one of contempt or admiration. Time would tell. Clark was a good match for Mark Turner's eloquence. His sturdy Midwestern nuances contrasted just enough with Mark's somewhat stilted cadence.
"Doctor" Clark began in what was now somewhat repetitive medico-legal introduction" you don't really believe this was all just 'an unfortunate event' do you?"
"Yes, I think that was as probable as any other explanation."
"And what would that 'other explanation be?" "That it was human error"
"Doctor, we have heard considerable testimony thus far. Something seemed to go wrong a the termination of that procedure. Do you not agree?"
"I am not certain we can say 'something' went wrong. The proof just not there."
Please, doctor. We cannot be back at the surgical suite at the precise moment when this occurred, obviously. But it does seem as if the evidence points in that direction."
":I cannot agree it does with any certainty."
Clark seemed to gradually come to the conclusion that there was not much more to say. It was time to send this to the critics-the jury.

And so it was. The judge went through his scripted routine to be certain there was no more questions. It was late in the day so he decided that all would return on the following day when the jury would deliberate the case. Frank was both disappointed and somewhat relieved. He wanted, obviously, to get this over as quickly as possible but at the same time remained somewhat apprehensive about the outcome. Should he? Well, now we will wait until tomorrow as the play rolls on to its... whatever fucking conclusion.

Donnaldson rose and told Frank he to meet him in the corridor. He turned to Carol and waited until she could join him as they left the courtroom.

"I thought it went rather well, honey' she told him I as reassuring voice as she could muster.: "Who the hell knows."

"I know, Frank but still I think the jurors seemed sympathetic." "How in the world can you tell, honey?" he asked

"Well, let's just say its my female intuition."

He smiled broadly. He was watching as the jury filed out. He was trying to see if any were turning to take a last look at him before they left for the day. None did.

Meeting up with Donnaldson just outside the courtroom, Frank and Carol both seemed eager to get his read on the day's events.

"Well, counselor, what is your take?"

"Good, very good Frank. I think we have them thinking it may well have been just 'one of those things' that could not really be prevented or if not, it was not your doing."

"So now we just wait until tomorrow to see what the critics say I guess" Frank rather glumly intoned

"Yes, yes, doctor. Don't be so pessimistic. I think all will be fine."

"We certainly hope so" Carol added. She had noticed how Donnaldson would give her one of those 'nice chick' glances from time to time. Well, good, she thought. Maybe the jurors will feel the same. I guess that was my role anyway.

As the three of them started to turn to go out the building, Ken and Kopsberg walked by. Ken nodded to Frank and Carol.

"Ken," Frank hastily called" I think things are going to be all right. I really do."

He nodded again and walked out without saying a word. Frank glanced at Carol but Donnaldson quickly threw in his appraisal. 'He is a young guy who is getting a too early introduction to the world of legal medicine, Frank. I think he is a bit stunned. He'll be fine after tomorrow."

Frank nodded and hoped that he certainly would be. Hopefully, so will I. he thought.

The three of them walked down the flight of marble steps leading out of the courthouse to the street. It was a gorgeous day, a bit cool, but sunny with just a hint of wind. Unusual for Chicago this time of year. Donnaldson pointed out, particularly here where the courthouse is situated. He told them to have a comfortable evening and he would see them back at 9:00 the next morning. He wanted to be sure both of them were visible to the jurors if they had a chance to be in the courtroom with them before they adjourned for their deliberations.

The drive home was more melancholy than any Frank had taken in years. His world was still intact but seemed ready to crumble. He knew all the stuff about how being sued was 'part of doing business' but this seemed more. It dug into his very innards, setting off a maelstrom of mixed emotions. The wall that had surrounded him since he could remember, that wall of confidence and security seemed on the edge of falling. His utter belief in himself as a very good, not just good, surgeon and physician was on the precipice. What happens if all of that disappears? He thought he had the emotional armor to handle this but he wasn't doing a very good job and he sensed it. As it turned out, so did Carol.

"Frank. Don't be so quiet. Tell me what you're thinking and how you feel after all of this crap today?"
"Like shit, honey. Like total shit. I know doctors get sued all of the time but when it's you, it hurts. It really hurts. I know that a lot of these lawsuits are bull shit and should never see the light of day. Lawyers have to eat too. Whether this one should even have brought is, I guess, still a question. I feel really bad for Harriet Johnson. I really do. I don't think any of us that day did anything wrong but I can't be sure, of course. I know I didn't and that should give me peace but it really hasn't. I hate pointing the finger at Ken and he doesn't seem to be handling this well. I don't know what will happen to him if they find us culpable."
"They won't honey. But…" and she hesitated before asking the next question. "Can they find you innocent and Ken guilty of malpractice?"
"I guess. I don't really know. Never did ask Donnaldson. Stupid not to but I just didn't." "Well, I don't think either of you will be. I think they will say it was nobody's fault"

He squeezed her hand and drove silently for the next several miles. The surrounding, while quite familiar and satisfying in the Fall seemed to be the fauna on another planet. Finally, they turned into their drive and went into the house.

Terri and Tim met them at the entrance from the garage. It seemed that it had been years since Carole had seen them although it was just that morning.

"Hi kids" Frank exclaimed. It was a rather typical greeting that parents throw at their children. But to Frank, this seemed to be an entrance into a better world than he had been in. One of more innocence and promise.

"OK, dad" Tim pounced" how did it go today. Teri and I have been really kinda worried."

Carole and Frank exchanged glances, each with a smile that only parents really know. Frank knew he needed to both console and reassure their children. They really did not have any concept of all of this and maybe thought their father would go to jail. He should have been more explicit before all of this.

"Well, kids, rather well. I think dad's going to be just fine."

Teri, in all of her sweet innocence, put her arms around him and fairly shouted her delight

"Oh Daddy you mean we can still live here and you can still be a doctor?"

That stunned Carole. She had no idea that they had been quite this bothered. They obviously knew something was afoot as both she and Frank tried to explain what it was all about but they seemed to accept even that most shallow of explanations and went about their lives as children of this age normally do.

"Of course, Teri. Goodness, it really isn't about any of that. Sometimes bad things can happen to people when they are sick. You know how you feel when things aren't right. Sometimes you just want to blame someone or something for all of it even though you know it had nothing to do with them. Well, this is a little like that. Daddy deals with those kind of problems but some times his patient is angry about how things went and this is how they take out their anger. Can you understand that?"

Teri looked at her mother with just a traced of tears streaming down her face. "I think so, Mommy. But everyone is okay now, right?"

"Right."

Frank just stared at all of three of them. The drama seemed to be continuing and he could not control Shit, this this goddamn thing is driving me nuts. Why can't I accept it like so many others seemed to be able to do.

"Well." Carole said finally, let's have dinner. I made a nice roast like you all like this morning and now, we are going to have it! How does that sound?"

"Great, mom" Tim fairly shouted.

"Good idea. Honey." Frank chimed in,.hoping to insert a patina of normalcy to the seeming lunacy of this day.

They sat down to a dinner of roast meat, twice-baked potatoes, mixed vegetables and a gigantic salad that Carole had also prepared that morning. She had always insisted on that salad but tonight it seemed especially welcomed to all four of them. Again, that touch of normalcy

"Dad, what is it like to be..." Teri hesitated to finish the sentence. "In a trial ?"

"I guess"

"Well. Like sitting to take a test and the questions have little to do with what you have studied. Does that make sense?"

Teri seemed to take a moment to digest his analogy, rolling it through her young mind to incorporate it into the experience he just described.

"I think so, dad. That would make me kinda scared." "Me too" Tim chimed in.

"Well, it was and still is kinda scary. Listen, let me set all of this straight. I am a doctor, after all, so I need to put all of this in some perspective for you two. When you do what I do, especially what I do, human s are not quite like machines. Things can go wrong when you least expect it. Sometimes it is the fault of the doctor and sometimes it just happens. So, there is a system out there that seeks to make doctors, me, supposedly more careful and if you make a mistake you should not have, you will be responsible to make up that mistake to the patient or to their family. That is called 'malpractice' and that is where all of those lawyers get involved. That is what I have been involved in now for the past several months. But I feel and so does my lawyer that I did nothing wrong. no mistakes were made that I could control and that this was one of those things that just 'happens'." "So, you just go on doing what you always do, right?" Tim asked

"Yes, Just like I have been doing. Everything should be fine for all of us."

They finished the meal as Carol gradually was able to shift the conversation from the courtroom drama to the events that shaped their children's life. She felt confident that they felt secure once more. She also had that feeling of satisfaction. Yes, her husband was right. Everything g was going to be all right and they would go on just as they had.

But Frank did not have that feeling. He could not get the picture of Harriet Thompson out of his head. There was no question she was not the woman she was before the surgery. He still felt comfortable that he had nothing to do with it but her appeal the critics-the jury was hard to estimate. Would they feel that the woman was owed her due regardless of whether or not he or Ken had anything to do with that outcome?

Frank made a point to be with both Teri and Tim that night. No calls, no reading of any medical literature. Just the four of them, gathered around the television and watching whatever any one of them chose. He lit the fireplace and with the chill in the Fall air it sent a aura of warm serenity and safety over the room.

That night, in the security of their bed, Carol asked him if he felt as confident as she did about the outcome.
"Yes and no. I think both Kopsberg and Donnaldson were effective. But that Clark guy is pretty damn good. And, really, honey it is the sight of Harriet, that beautiful but forlorn woman that creeps me out. How many of those jurors feel she deserves something remains to be seen. It is a hell of a play though. It rally is. We the actors going through our parts with the critics watching and listening, making their critical judgments. I have no fucking idea how this thing will turn. Play out. One or five stars."
"C'mere, you' she beckoned 'let me heal all those worry warts"
And they sank into a rather passionate fit of sex, trying to erase all signs of the hours that had just passed. It was quite therapeutic to him but it did not remove the dread that had settled over him about tomorrow.

CHAPTER FIFTEEN

The walk up those marble stairs to the room that Frank called the 'theatre' was now familiar. Too familiar. The Courthouse was beginning to ignite with activity. He wondered what was going on in the other rooms. Could there be other guys like him in the same predicament? Curious. Taking a deeper breath than he thought necessary, he entered the room. Donnaldson was already seated in his familiar spot, browsing through a copy of the Tribune. Looking up and seeing them he quickly arose from the chair.

"Frank, Frank, Right on time as usual. And Carole, as beautiful as usual." "Good morning, Alan. I see you are dressed to kill again."

Donnaldosn didn't know whether to take that as a compliment or a mild rebuke. He chose the former. "Thank you, doctor. I believe the appearance can move the critics."

Neither Frank nor Carole responded to that. It was past that stage he imagined. So here we are, he thought. The nightmare of all doctors. The dreaded courtroom with your reputation on the line, Forget the monetary awards. The dagger to the heart that these things cause is as bad as he imagined it would be. Fuck, what did happen that day? I'll never know. Let's just hope the critics don't either, or at least, don't think they know enough to blame us. Hope. Hope

He watched as the proceedings got under way. Again, the glance at Ken. The return glance was hard to fathom. He had hardly spoken to him since all this began. He really did not know if Ken thought he had planned to use him as his shield against defeat. No matter. It was done.

The judge began his dissertation to the jurors about deciding the case. The usual, Donnaldson assured him. The, one by one they filed out to the juror's room, the 'critic's hatch' as Donnaldson called it.
Frank took time to look around the room. Familiar and unfamiliar faces. Do people come to these things just to watch he wondered. He knew there was a reporter for the Tribune that had been at the hearings since they began. Big time stuff these things he thought. "So what do we do now?" Carole asked.

"Wait, my dear" Donnaldson replied rather unctuously

"Here?" Frank cut in.

"Well, have you eaten already?" "Some."
"Well, let's go grab some coffee. Would you like to ask Dr. Laser to join us?"

Frank had only perfunctorily spoken to Ken over that past few days. But, still, he truly liked him and admired him, despite what he seemingly had to do in his own defense. Would this gesture help with… anything? Maybe.

"Sure" he finally responded. "I think I need to feel comfortable with him again." Donnaldson glanced over at the desk where Ken and Sam Kopsberg were sitting. "Listen, do you want to include Sam or what?'

"Doubt you can separate them" Frank answered "Sure, let him join us if he and Ken want to." "Fine"

Donnaldson got up and walked over to Ken and Sam. Donnaldson was wearing a three button suit with a French-cuffed shirt with pearl cuff links. His tie was gathered in what Frank thought ws a perfect Windsor tie. Impressive son-of -a -bitch he thought. Maybe that stuff does sway the critics. He watched him speaking first to Sam following a handshake and then to Ken who looked impassively over to Frank.

As Donnalsdon returned, he was shaking his head in a positive manner. Well, okay, Frank thought. I'll try to use this to smooth a bit of this out for Ken and me.

"Yes, they both would like to join us for coffee. I suggested the Starbucks across the street. I am a entrenched Starbucks addict so I hope that meets your approval."

"Sure. I have no problem with that. Carole likes that stuff too. Latte and all of that."

Carole told them she did like 'all of that' and was happy Ken was coming. She knew him but had not really talked to him over the past several weeks and was anxious to see how he was holding up. She was aware of the Donnaldson strategy. He was such a sweet guy, at least that part of him she knew and this crap must be eating at him.

Frank, Carole and Donnaldson walked over to their table. "Hi Ken "Carole greeted him cheerfully.

Ken sat silently for a moment before replying. "Mrs. Martin. Good to see you. Not so much in this setting but always glad to have you around."

"Well, thank you. You know what Frank and I think about you."

Frank wasn't certain that was the appropriate thing to say… He watched Ken's face screw up just enough to send a mild chill through him. When Ken did not respond to that his anxiety level started rising. May be it wasn't a good idea to have them join us, he thought. Oh what the hell. This all may turn out just fine. I do not need to feel guilty about him. No reason. Just none.

But they all walked out together into the brilliant Fall sunshine. The street was bustling with people coming and going into the Courthouse. Cars were streaming by in an endless caravan. They needed to cross a block away as the Starbucks was on a side street.

"This place is always jam packed." Donnadlson said. "Let's hope we can get a table. Some of the young lawyers hit it for the opportunity to bullshit with each other and some like the computer friendly atmosphere, Me? I just like the coffee. That awesome coffee."

It was as he described. Shoulder to shoulder, the line for coffee and the assorted variations of it stretching towards the door. Somehow, Kopsberg spotted a table that was just emptying and he grabbed it.

"Ken and I will sit while you three get the coffee. Is that okay?"

"Sure" Carole quickly answered. It seemed she was trying to be bearer of good tidings, trying to make certain all of this went smoothly. She asked what he and Ken wanted and quickly moved to take her place in line, Frank and Donnaldson trailing behind. Frank was impressed. He sensed her mission and was relieved she was doing this.

"Thanks" he whispered to her. "For what?"
"Being you."

"Well, thanks, but I'm not certain why that came out."

She knew, of course and was comfortable with it. Reaching the front of the line, she placed the orders except for Donnaldson's.

"Me? I take a great big cup of the strongest coffee they can come up with. No sugar, no cream, just hot, challenging coffee."

The three of them gathered all of the orders, including Carole's cherished latte and returned to the table that Sam had claimed. The five of them then did the consummate dance of weaving and bobbing. Sma ll talk dominated the conversation until Alan turned the ship around.

"Well, *Sam*" he began looking directly at Kopsberg with a subtle glance at Ken, "what is your take on all of this?"

Frank looked quickly at Carole who returned his gaze with an expression of uncertainty.

Even Ken had now tightened, seemingly growing more intense with this wave that had suddenly overflowed all of them.

"Mrs. Johnson is an impressive picture of the archetypical injured party demanding justice."

With that Frank felt as if his world had collapsed. Simple. Just as Alan had said, the critics may not pay much attention to the facts but only to what they see on that screen. And Kopsberg had probably nailed it. The innocent party who had been injured by forces unknown but to whom one owes something. Something. Not just pity but revenge perhaps on the system that had allowed this to happen. Even if that system ws Nature itself. And Frank and Ken were part of a System. That great system of Medicine. Nobel beyond doubt but still part of the human experience, not to be totally divorced from it, of course.

"And you think she will alone sway the decision?"

"I am not certain. But I think so. I tend to agree that this was an act of God, if you will, just something that happened. But" and here he paused just enough for emphasis" my client seems to have been put in a more tenuous position than yours."

Well, okay. It was out in the open now. Frank held his breath and did not want to reply. His anxiety grew as

Donnaldson hesitated. But thankfully, responded quickly enough to prevent the level of tension from rising too far.

"First, I think the critics will go beyond the physical appearance of Harriet Johnson and go for the facts. Just a hunch. And if not, I am not certain whose position is more tenuous."

"I hope your first statement is correct." And that was the extent of the discussion of the case as the mood lifted slightly with more small talk which even included Ken's inquiry into the status of Tim and Terri.

"Well" Donnaldson finally declared" I think it is time we meander back to the Courtroom. Maybe a bit early but still, we should be there.

Frank and Carole were relieved to step out into the warmth of the Sun once more. It seemed tio penetrate enough to sooth the friction that this meeting had created. Probably a mistake, Frank thought, to do this but, what the fuck, at least Ken knows we are not ignoring him. He debated whether to say more to him before they reentered the courtroom. He moved alongside him now, turned and told him that he hoped everything would turn out well for both of them.

"Yeh. This has been a pain in the ass, Frank. I haven't been able to do my stuff too well for weeks now. That ain't good."

Frank was pleased at the mildly friendly response and the fact he called him by his first name. He eally did like this guy and hoped, really hoped, the verdict was good for them both. He hated to use the defense he had but that was the way the world moved for him now.

"Same here, really. Sorry we haven't been able to work more together. Maybe after this is all over with."

"Better the way it is."

That shook Frank. Obviously, Ken was already bitter. And this before any verdict. Shit.
He did not talk any further with Ken. He felt a bit sad about their relationship or the end of it perhaps. When Carole asked him about it he merely told her there was not that much to tell. Better to leave it at that.

The courtroom seemed more dismal than ever. Too massive, it seemed, for matters like this. Frank and Carole took their seats, she still behind him and Donnaldson. Frank wasn't certain if what happenend next was a good or bad sign but the jury was ready to return.

"Well, well." Donnaldson said" look how soon they are returning. Most unusual." "What in the hell does that mean?" Frank asked
"Don't know. They decided that one pretty quickly. Can mean good can mean bad."

"Great." Frank responded with some trepidation. He felt his pulse quicken and his palms moisten. He wasn't used to this tension, even in the middle of some of his most demanding surgical procedures.

The judge asked for the verdict to be delivered to him which was done by someone who did those things Frank figured. Now, the wait, the fucking wait for the answer. Then it came.

"The jury has found for the plaintiffs. They believe the primary negligence was by Dr. Laser but Dr. Martin is also culpable as he was the leading surgeon. The plaintiffs are asking for an award of two million dollars which was also approved by the jury."

There was muted applause and high fives over at the table of the Johnsons. They had won.

Frank sat stunned. His breathing actually grew labored. He glanced over at Ken who seemed even more stunned. While his defense had worked to some extent he still felt miserable about this. What would this do to Ken?

"Sorry, Frank. I really thought we were safe" Donnaldson told him. "I think they made a mistake but…" "Can we appeal?" Carole inquired.

"No. no. Difficult to appeal these malpractice suits. Mrs. Thompson was just too appealing to the critics. That was our concern. Facts? Remember they may not count here. It's the movies and she was a superstar, so to speak. But, you are still a doctor, Frank, you can still do your thing. So, as much as this may hurt, and I am sure it does, your life goes on. This really doesn't reflect on your competence whatsoever. So you will get over this sooner than you think. I feel you have a strong ego which can handle it."

Frank tried to process all of this stuff. Yeh, life goes on but how do I handle this? How does poor Ken handle this? The future now began to look more bleak than he had ever felt in his life. He had accepted the fact that something had went wrong in that operating room. He just did not know, really, what that something was. Did Ken really screw up? He continued to drill into himself the absolute certainty that hedid nothing wrong. But that just did not remove the stain of this and the sting. The goddamn sting. It just cut right to his heart. Does any doctor really mean to screw up? He doubted it but sometimes screwing up does happen. But he didn't think this was one of those times. At least as far as hews concerned.

Ken? Maybe. Maybe. But he just didn't know. He's really never really know. But this was how the system worked in this country. No question avenues need to exist to correct injustices. But this play? This assembly of critics? No knowledge, really, of what goes on in that operating room. Bad results maybe but true malpractice? True negligence even? Was there a way to separate them? He did not know. Only that the system had ripped his heart out. For now. Could he recover? Could that steely self confidence be restored? That self-confidence that every surgeon really needs to do what a surgeon does. And Ken? So goddamn young, So fucking young. No, neither of them would go to jail or anything like that, of course. But it seemed that the verdict was like a sentence to go down the road of self doubt and blame and guilt. Not a good spot for anyone. Particularly for a doctor and a surgeon.

CHAPTER SIXTEEN

He was back in that room now. Its emptiness eerie and foreboding. It had been over ten years since that day but it was forever etched in his memory, like some tune that never truly leaves your consciousness. The marble floor, still gleaming in its cleanliness. The row of seats where the 'critics' had sat and gave their read on the play that had just been presented to them. He could almost remember every face of that cast.

He sat down in the same chair that he had occupied throughout the proceedings. It felt as if he had just sat in it. He remembered his feelings after the judgment of the critics had been given. Donnaldson's cheerful reassurance that this was certainly not the end of his life, not the end of his career, just a' bump in the road'. He remembered his colleagues a the hospital the first day he returned after the trial He could almost recall, word by word, Gary Larson's comments, once again, that this was the 'price of doing business, part of a surgeon's baggage.' But it was not just a 'bump in the road'. There was this perception he had that his fellow surgeons, particularly those in cardiovascular surgery, acted just a bit differently than they had before. Carole tried to reassure him that this was just his imagination and how many of them have been or will be involved in this stuff themselves? He told himself that surely she was right. Maybe it was his imagination but he could just not shake it. And he drifted off to a night three weeks after this all happened. He had come home fairly early for him and found Tim already back from school. "Hi dad" he had greeted him with that flourish of adolescence that always gave Frank some sense of delight and wonder. "you are sure home early today. Everything OK?"

"Yea, sure Tim. Everything is fine. You know this was my day in the office. Got through my patients rather quickly and was able to jump over the hospital and make sure every thing was smooth there."

The truth was that he had just a few surgical procedures in the time period since he returned to his practice full time. Part of that was deliberate. He could not schedule any until he knew it was over. But he also sensed that maybe the flow of patients had slowed. Was it possible that the publicity, including that story in the ***Chicago Tribune*** had really bothered potential referrals? He thought he was still regarded as one of the best in the Chicago area. His confidence had slipped a little but he thought he was doing a satisfactory job in restoring it. He wasn't sure his attitude would ever be the same but he also felt his skills, which he never doubted, remained quite intact. He had talked to one of his most trusted colleagues, Doug Baker, who had indeed been involved in a malpractice suit that went on much longer and in which the verdict also went against him.

"Oh, shit, Frank" he had confided to him one day in the surgeons' lounge "yea it hurts a little but you and I know a lot of this stuff is all bullshit. Bunch of hungry and greedy lawyers trying to make a better living. Wanting their Lamborghinis and a condo on the ocean. We're their ticket to some of that. But, the insurance company, the 'deep pockets' as they are apparently known in the lawyer business, came though for me with all bells ringing. You'll get over it, buddy. I'll probably get sued again. Yea, it's part of the business. But we cannot stop doing what we are do because of that threat. I think I do a hell of a job in repairing some of nature's mistakes and I know you do.

Dangerous business in a way, isn't it. So may things can go wrong. But we do our fucking best to avoid that one little bitty mistake that costs so much damage to a lot of people I guess. I try my hardest not to let that thought stay with me. We could not do what we have to do if we did. And to tell you the truth, Frank, I love what I do."

That was one hell of pep talk, Frank had thought and thanked him for his insights and understanding. It did play a role in his slow recovery from the shock of that day. He did not think Donnaldson was 'one of those greedy lawyers' that Doug had implicated. He liked him. Thought he did his best and through all of this, Frank continued to believe that some system needed to in place to protect those who had indeed suffered a true 'malpractice' if you will, a real mistake. They happen, Frank knew that. But he still did not believe he had made one.

"I'm just not used to seeing you home at this time, Dad' Tim told him.

"Well, once in awhile it is a treat for me."

"Yea, I guess it would be. Well, for once, it's my turn to tell a neat little tidbit."

Frank eyed him like all parents do when their child seems to be on that cusp of adulthood. With some awe and pride and bit of skepticism.

"And what might that be.?"

"Well, I aced my biology test today. Not just aced, Dad, got the highest grade in class."

Frank high-fived his beaming son. For a moment, he did forget that day in court. It was a welcome reprieve. "Terrific. I would not expect a son of a surgeon to do any less. And for a reward for this brilliant young man standing before me, I offer two 40 yard tickets to watch the Bears this Sunday."

All of this was repeated when Carole returned from a shopping trip and Teri came in from her basketball practice.

"Dad. You know I like football too. Why can't I go?" Carole smiled at the insouciance of her young daughter. Very much like her father, tough and determined.

"Why not indeed?"

"Done, little lady. I will do my very best to get... well, how about four tickets?"

"Yes!" Tim blurted "we've never gone to a Bears game as a family."

They settled down to one of the few family dinners Frank had enjoyed in weeks. It was filled with all the small talk that makes those kinds of dinners what they are. It was rather therapeutic. The evening sun, dipping in the West, projected the shadows of all four of them like a kaleidoscope on then walls. Frank felt like this might be like the ball that predicted the future, a better one than he had been able to imagine over the past several weeks. Then the telephone rang. A ring that would strike him like a bolt of lightening, forever hurdling him into what the future was really to be. The ring of the damned.

Frank answered as he often did as the call frequently was for him. He was in a generally good mood when he picked up the phone.

"Frank?"

"Yes, this is Frank. Who... wait a minute, gee, it's you Karl isn't it?"

"Yes."

Karl was Karl Green, Chief of Cardiovascular Surgery at Northwestern whose Service he did most of his procedures.

"Frank. I wanted to be the one who told you."

"Told me what, Karl?" "Ken. Ken Laser." "What about Ken?"

"He shot himself this afternoon, Frank, He fucking shot and killed himself today."

That moment would be forever etched in his memory. It was truly one of those turning points that can change the lives of even the most stable of us.

"Frank? Frank? Are you there?" Karl implored.

Frank was so stunned he could not answer that question for more seconds than he realized. Finally:

"Yes, uh, yes, Karl... I..."

"I know how fond of Ken you were, Frank, and, of course, we all know he was part of that trial you just under went. Now, I know you are going to feel guilty about this. I just know you will. I ant you to come in first thing in the morning to my office. I have no surgeries scheduled and neither do you. I want to talk to you, Frank. You are too good of a surgeon to let this bother you and I want to be of help. OK?"

No answer.

Frank? Listen, as your chief I am requesting your presence in my office tomorrow morning at 8:00 sharp. Is that clear?"

Frank was still trying to distill what he just been told. Stunned was too mild a word for his emotions. But he had to answer.

"Yes… I'll… see you tomorrow morning, Karl. Tomorrow… morning."

"Good. Please, Frank, don't do anything rash and keep that appointment?"

"I will… I mean I won't and I will."

Hanging up that phone brought a new rush of confusing emotions. Ken. Ken had killed himself. That smart, promising young guy… had killed himself! Oh my God. He thought. He walked uncertainly back to the dinner table. Carole, of course, had sensed, as most wives tend to do, the rapid change in his mood.

"Honey, who was that?"

"Ken. Ken Laser… He…" pausing. Frank simply was frozen at that point. His body seemed out of sync, disconnected to the reality in front of him.

"What about Ken ?Frank, what in the hell is wrong. Please?"

Both Tim and Teri sat rather stunned. Not knowing what to make of this. All they knew was that the joviality of the moment had been shattered by some terrifying and mysterious intrusion.

Finally, he was able to sit back down in the chair. Staring out in space, he forced himself to answer.

"Ken Laser shot himself."

The silence that followed was like a ethereal cloud that paralyzed all of them.

Finally, Carole stood up, walked over to him, and as he placed her arms around his neck, summoned up words that seemed to be part of the cloud.

"Oh, Jesus, Frank. Ken? Your prize resident? That sweet sweet kid?"

"Yeh. That sweet, sweet kid. My prize resident. He shot himself, Carole. The son- of- a -bitch shot himself!"

Tim, stunned as any adolescent would be in that unreality, searched for what his reaction should be. He knew that Ken Laser was a trainee working with his father and was also involved in the trial that he had hoped was behind them. "Dad... is... he dead?"

Carole who by now had allowed the emotions to emerge was quietly crying as she rubbed her husband shoulders. Frank felt so inadequate in trying to respond to his son. He truly felt shattered but wanted to convey some sort of control and reassurance to his son's obvious deep anxiety. "I think so, Timmy. But... yes, I think so."

"Why would he do that, Daddy?" Teri innocently probed. How would he answer such a direct but incredibly profound question like that?

"I'm a... not really sure, honey" he offered" I guess he was very, very depressed by all of this. Very" and then, to his dismay, lost control. The one thing he did not want to allow himself to do just now. Not in front of his two kids. Not now. But the emotions could not be stopped. Just couldn't be stopped. All of what had gone on before seemed to swell like a blister and burst in his mind. He began to sob like he had not done in... God, forever.

Carole tightened her grip on him, "Kids, this is just an awful awful thing. Ken... was" she tried to compose herself through her own emotional earthquake ":one of your father's favorite trainees. God... why... why..."

Teri had never seen her parents quite like this. She always had that vision of him being like granite stone, strong and immobile in the face of any dangers, the dashing surgeon

123

who she worshipped. And now, to see him like this tore at her young soul, devastatingly.

"Daddy. Is… there anything… Tim and I can do for you? Please tell us how we can help."

Was this not a scene played out a million times over a thousand years. Children witnessing the utter emotional distress of their parents. Helplessness, all-pervasive helplessness, is the omnipresent emotion.

Frank finally gained whatever control over himself that he could. He arose from the chair, walked over to Teri, and took her in his arms. The comfort of the innocence of children can be self-curative, "Just be yourselves, kids. This is just such a shock to me and your Mother. I don't want this to get in your way. OK?"

He knew, of course, that that was a silly request but one that one must utter at times like this. It will get in their way, he thought, and it sure as hell will get in mine.

CHAPTER SEVENTEEN

It was, as he expected, one of the most fitful nights he had ever spent. Why he even tried to sleep escaped him, aside from the fact that surgeons are supposed to get 'a good nights rest' Carole fared no better. Frank thought that whomever said the night can be filled with terror was certainly correct The thoughts rolled around like a repetitive wave. He felt those tinges of guilt manifested by dry mouth and a feeling of wet palms he had hardly ever experienced those before, even in the throes of some of his most demanding surgeries. Did his and Dannenberg's defense approach take too much of a toll? Did he feel so personally responsible that he killed himself? Malpractice suits, they tell, us over and over, are 'part of doing business' and often relate to just a bad outcome without any personal malfeasance. He had tried to believe that and was convincing himself that indeed this was the often the case. But this... this.

"Honey, you have just got to face this is a realistic way" she told him "I know this will eat at you. It's eating at me and I know a bit how you must feel. If you hold yourself personally responsible for what Ken did, you will never be a peace"

Frank simply stared at the ceiling. He felt as if he was being thrown from one unwelcome thought to the other.

"Frank, honey? Are you all right?" "No."
"Well, that was an honest answer"
"Oh crap, Carole. This is awful. Just fucking awful. I really just want to cry" "Do it"
He drew her to him and buried his head into her breasts. She felt the drops as he quietly began to sob, Carole tried to control her own emotions. She had rarely seen her husband like this. The strong, confident surgeon was melting before her eyes. How to help him? Only when his mother had died during his last year of residency did he exhibit these emotions. Would this be even worse than that? She could not imagine it would but the element of his personal involvement here was upsetting.

"His parents..." he started in an interrupted, halting fashion, 'How... do I talk to them?" "I know, I know. I. that will be hard. But, Frank, you have just got to get to the point where you do not feel so personally guilty about what happened."
"But I do. Oh God, I do."

He laid quietly in her arms throughout the rest of that terrifying night. Maybe a few moments of sleep, maybe not. He had really never felt quite like this before. Finally, the first few beams of sunlight crept through the window shades. Removing the darkness helped some. Not much, though. He went through his usual morning routine. Thank goodness for the mechanical parts of our lives as he could not really focus on much else besides the events of last night. He just still could not believe that that young,

promising man had really killed himself! Killed himself1
He absolutely did not feel like eating but knew he should at
least have a cup of coffee, knowing what would happen if
he missed his 'caffeine fix' He did not wait until, either Teri
or Tim came to the kitchen. He spotted Carole in her robe
approaching him with, no doubt, words of encouragement
or whatever.

"Talk to Karl, honey. He's a good guy. Let some of the stuff
out."

"Sure. Let it out. Well, we'll see, honey. The road to
salvation lies somewhere I'm sure. I just don't know where
to start looking."

He kissed her and somewhat spontaneously took her
in his arms for one of the more enduring hugs she had
experienced from him. God, what can I do for this man?
My strong, guy. My really good, caring surgeon who is
falling apart before my very eyes?

He slowly left her arms and picked up his keys to the car.
Drying the tears, also a shock to him, he nodded good-
bye and started the drive, once more, to the hospital and
his meeting with Karl Green. This drive was clearly one
of the most melancholy he could remember. He found
the surround dings a bit soothing, probably because of
their familiarity and reassurance that his life hadn't yet
totally imploded. It was early fall and the trees were just
starting to slowly exhibit those spectacular colors that
only nature seemingly can do. This was one of the times
he enjoyed being in the Mid-west., But he just could not
get the thought of Ken's suicide out of his mind. It tore
into him like a hot iron, relentlessly burning its way into
his consciousness. How would he feel walking into that

hospital now? What would they say to him? Hopefully, he could slip up to Karl's office without being noticed.

He decided to take the back stairs to the fourth floor where Karl's office sat, hoping to avoid a potentially crowded elevator... The office was, fortunately, adjacent to the stairwell. It was just after 8:00 but Karl was never on time. He opened the door and finding no one else in the anteroom, took a chair and grabbed a nearby magazine to shield himself should anyone else entered. He did not know why he was so self-conscious but he was.

The office was in keeping with Karl's character: wood paneled elegance softened with art work reflecting his keen interest in sailing. Various sized boats with intriguing sails were cleverly placed about the panels, creating an atmosphere of oceanic serenity. He had only a few moments, regretfully he felt, to just sit in this cave of escape until Karl opened the door to his office and motioned to him to come in.

Karl Green was the personification of a man whose personality gushed with vitality and warmth. Medium height but built in a sturdy New England fashion reflecting his Ver mont background, he sported a well kept beard, whitened a bit by age, but giving him a respectful but reassuring visage. He had always been one of Frank's favorite people and a really good and reliable Department Head.

"Frank, how good to see you. Not the way I wanted to but... please do come in."

He ushered him into his inner office. Again, the wood paneling blended in with his projection of stability and strength.

"Please sit down" he asked him as he pointed to a large leather chair facing a desk that was large by Frank's standards and covered with a swamp of papers anchored to some extent by a rather large sailboat that served as a paper holder.

A moment silence preceded any further remarks by Karl.

"Just a total bunch of crap, isn't it?" he asked him.

Usually, Karl had a whiff of insouciance about him, even with the major of problems but he seemed very serious right now. Close to sixty, Frank surmised, his face had the weatherized appearance of someone who enjoys the outdoors. He knew he sailed his boat as often time permitted on Lake Michigan He was an ardent tennis player. And extremely well read as well and an excellent surgeon to boot. Frank's version of the 'renaissance man'

"Yea, Karl. Total crap."

"Where do I start?" he asked him

"Anywhere" Frank answered.

"Well, first of all, you are aware that Ken was in the special surgical program outside of the usual residency."

"Yes, I think I knew that. Why is that important now?"

Well, it he was in the usual training slot he would have not been sued." Frank looked at him incredulously. "What in the hell do you mean?"

"Residents, that is, those in our regular program would not have been sued. The hospital would be. It's a part of the liability chain."

He was just not aware of that. Why hadn't Donnaldson or any of the other attorneys told him that? Maybe they thought I knew. Did Ken know? Certainly he must have.

"Karl, did Ken know this?"

"Yes. He knew there were three in the special program and that he could be sued as an individual physician not under the auspices of the hospital."

Frank sat very quite as he let this information permeate his thoughts. Ken could have avoided the suit if he had not entered the special program.

"Karl, he might still be alive if he hadn't chosen to come into that program." "Well, yes and no. He chose to exit the standard program to get more exposure and work and…" he hesitated for just the briefest of moments "to be able to be your assistant as much as he did. He would not have done that on the standard residency track."

Ifhe did not think he could not have drifted further into this blue state of semi depression he knew now that he could. So Ken wanted to work more with him. And he threw him under the fucking bus. Shit.

Karl Green was well known for his incredible ability to size a situation up rapidly and act accordingly. He was one of the most highly respected surgeons in the hospital and, as a matter of fact, in the city. Tough but very honest. A born listener who was not paral yzed by the other persons words, Frank knew he would be sympathetic but realistic.

"Frank. I know you will feel personally responsible for Ken's death. I do not know why this affected him like that. I cannot tell you how shocked I was to hear he did what he did. Did I think it was possible? My honest answer? No. Ken seemed like one of the most solid young surgeons we had. There was no hint of any underling psychological quirk that I would suspect this to be possible. None that I knew of. We could have a long discourse here on the liability system we have in this country. I know you are in no mood to hear a lecture on malpractice. But here, it is important. For a bunch of reasons We need to go over a few points. No lecture, Frank, just something you and I need to think about? OK?"

"Of course, Karl. No problem."

"First of all, Frank. You are one of the most gifted cardiovascular surgeons I know. I just don't want any of this getting in you way. You are too valuable a commodity for the medical world to lose"

"Thank you. I needed that."

"I am going to be as serious as I can be, Frank. I know you've heard some of this before. This stuff is a risk of doing business and all that. It is but necessary stuff. I don't know just how one constructs an ideal system to protect the patient as well as the doctor. Don't know. This probably isn't the best we have now but it's what it is. It will happen to a whole bunch of docs, particularly surgeons. You know that. Some of those lawyers out there are truly vultures. Not all of them, mind you. But enough to make the business a murky one sometimes. Defensive medicine and all that., Not that defensive medicine is all bad. We need to remind ourselves that we don't have a completely free hand to do whatever we want without considering the consequences. Does all of us some good. Up to a point. Yes, the word malpractice is bandied about somewhat carelessly times. We all have to deal with the unexpected bad outcomes of the decisions we make. The decisions the patient often makes with us. No one can prevent the bad outcomes. It is and has been and always will be part of medicine. Sometimes it is due to negligence. But sometimes that is not easy to prove and there is the rub. I am quite familiar with the Johnson case. I do not think there was provable negligence. I just don't. But this is the system we have to contend with. I am aware that these things can significantly affect one's psyche. I am not sure the public realizes that. We do shake it off eventually but it bites for a while. Makes us feel inadequate and cuts into our confidence. That is one bad part of it. A really bad part for the docs. This must have hit Ken really, really hard. It was his first suit but… it probably would not have been his last. I have never been involved with someone who killed himself over a guilty verdict. It has truly, truly shaken me. I am generally a tough ol' as you now, but this… this got to me. Really got to me. Almost everyone, I repeat, Frank, almost everyone gets over this stuff in due time. They realize it often has nothing to do with their competence and even if it does, they retread and make the adjustments and move on. I expect you to do the same, Frank. We need you, your patients need you, and the medical world needs you."

He stopped and rather sanguinely looked at Frank.

In return, Frank tried to appear more optimistic as if Karl's soliloquy hit the mark. It did and it didn't. He knew most of the things he heard was true but the fly in the ointment here was Ken's suicide. It changed everything, everything. He felt the best approach now was to respond somewhat in kind, to reassure Karl and be appreciate of what he had told him and of his carefully directed praise.

"I appreciate what you've said Karl, and I know you re right, of course. Yea, Ken's death has shook me up. That's an understatement. It'll take me longer to handle this but I will.

I think I'd like to take, maybe, a month off and let my soul heal. How does that sound?."

"I think that's fine, Frank. Do you have any pending surgeries.?"

"You know, just two and I can close my office stuff down now for a while so I don't schedule any more until I get back."

"Whatever is good for you. I just want you to come back raring to go with that old confidence and ability."

Frank smiled as best as he could. He stood up, shook Karl's hand and thanked him again and turned to walk out of his office. He still wanted to a avoid personal contacts for now but knew he had to see his hospital patients with the residents that afternoon. He couldn't duck this forever But first, he'd drive home and relax if he could for a few hours. He thought he might feel less depressed after meeting with Karl. But he didn't and the image of Ken Laser was implanted in his consciousness with even more intensity.

He was able to leave the hospital, again, without anyone he knew noticing him. Of course, it was unlikely anyone would have yet heard of Ken's death since it just happened but still, to him, it seemed that the entire world already knew. Even though he had to return in just a few hours, he wanted to be away from the place a bit more. He was relieved to get into his car but he sat in the seat not starting it for a few minutes trying to compose himself the best he could. It was not easy. He had never felt like this before. But, he would do what he had to do now, turned on the engine and drove out of the parking lot. Why driving a car could relax him remained a mystery to him but it did. So, on this trip it was almost therapeutic. The river of passing cars, the signs to streets with their all too familiar name inching him home, the slow loss of the skyline and then colors of the adjoining trees all, for whatever reason, seemed to sooth him. He was tempted to keep driving beyond his exit but decided it would be best no to and drove into his garage and as he opened the door saw Carole eagerly awaiting his report on the meeting with Karl Green.

"Well, honey, give me the low-down." "He was very supportive."

"I would have expected nothing less. Feel a b it better?"

Frank decided to portray a picture of coping. Better for everyone. But he wasn't and he knew it.

"Yes, I... think I do."

He spent the next two hours simply sitting in a chair, sipping coffee later with Carole, and giving her more detail about the meeting. He was certain she felt he would handle this. Then, he prepared for the drive back to the hospital and the first encounter with the aftermath of the death of Dr. Kenneth Laser.

CHAPTER EIGHTEEN

He wondered, as he again walked into the lobby of the hospital, why these immutable buildings seem to take on a different character after an event that alters your life. It was still the same hospital, the same immaculately cleaned white wall, the parades of photos of doctors past and present who had strode it's halls, and the peculiar odor that each hospital seems to own by itself. But it just was different now. He always, for some primordial reason, felt a sense of security behind these walls with their myriad collections of human triumph and tragedy. But he did not feel that way now On his way to the surgical post-operative suite a familiar face greeted him as the elevator doors opened, Alone, for now, at the back of the car was a tall, slim red-hair man wearing a white coat over his surgical green scrubs. His flaming red hair was unkempt but full., a pair of too large glasses sliding forward on his large Romanesque nose. He would stand out most anywhere, Frank thought, as he entered. Jerry Simmons, a brash but very competent urological surgeon with a twinkle in his eyes that advertised his gregarious nature.

"Frank" he literally bellowed. 'so good to see you. Listen fella, I was shocked to hear of Ken Laser's death. Fucking shocked. Do you know what the hell happened?"

"Hi Jerry." Frank seconded in as calm fashions he could muster. Sooner or later, he knew, he would have to confront this problem, these myriad questions. Might as well start with them right now,.

"No not really. He was a great guy and a very capable young surgeon." Frank thought that generic answer would have to do for now. He was not going to insert the malpractice suit if not asked

"That he was. Say, weren't you and him involved in some sort of suit recently?" Well, Frank thought, sooner rather than later. So be it.

"Yes. We were."

"I've heard that the outcome was not what you wanted."

"No it was not"

"Was that the problem with Ken?"

Frank knew that was going to be the natural progression of the Ken question. Face it now he told himself.

"You know, Jerry, I don't have all the info. I know he was upset about the trial, as we all would be, but I can't say much beyond that."

Larry Simmons was, in Franks pantheon of doctors, a veritable 'jerk' He really didn't care what he thought and he was going to leave the conversation at that.

"Well, I know how much you admired the guy. Sorry about it. Take care "He finished his sentence as he departed the elevator on the fourth floor, one floor below the cardiovascular unit.

The elevator door opened. He took a deep breath and walked onto the unit. The surroundings, again so familiar, seemed so foreign. Goddamn, this stuff was really starting to bother him. He slowly, fitfully, walked into the nursing station. Sitting behind a desk with a bank of screens was Evelyn Harris, one of the oldest nurses on the unit. Somewhat chunky, Evelyn had a keen sense of humor and irony and was very efficient.

In her mid-fifties, she had retained her youthful good looks "Good afternoon, Dr. Martin. A little. late for your rounds today, aren't you?"

"Hi Evelyn. Yes, I am. Had an important meeting this morning and a few items came up so, here I am… Anything I need to know?" A routine question he hoped would swing him back into the routine. And, had she heard about Ken? Probably, he thought. The grapevine in this place is faster than light.

She seemed to hesitate. Not sure if she should touch the issue? Hadn't really heard. But then.

"Yes, Mrs. Crawford in 219, Had a rough night. Fever up to 103 degrees and feeling a bit lousy."

Caroline Crawford was a fifty-four year old woman who had undergone an aortic valve replacement. The surgery went well and she had, up to now, done well. Ordinarily, he would have just pegged this up to a fairly routine postop fever. Now, a cough seemed to bother him.

"Any one seen her yet?"

"Well, we had called for Dr…" she stopped. "Doctor who?"

"She tried not to let her eyes meet his but answered in a hesitant, oblique manner.

"Well, Dr… Laser, of course. But when I did… well… they told me what had happened. Jesus, Dr. Martin, I just could not believe it. He was such a courteous and conscientious young man. I just…"

Frank felt as if a bolt of lightening had ran through him. This was what he would have to face from now on, at this hospital, in this town. The solid foundations of his life were crippling before him, like a pile of sand that was dispersing along the floor.

"Yes, he was, Evelyn, He certainly was. It was a tragic loss. Especially for me."

:I bet. I am truly sorry, Dr. Martin. Truly… I will miss him"

"Thanks. So will I." Frank responded without hesitation. He as truly sorry and truly would miss Kenneth Laser. But, somehow, life would go on. Or so he hoped.

Evelyn handed Frank Caroline Crawford's chart. He tried as hard as could to concentrate on what it told him but the image of Ken Laser seemed to be plastered throughout its pages. He put the chart down and stared off into space for a brief moment, looked at the chart again, and was able to appreciate the temperature curve and the notes of the night nurse and Evelyn.

Smiling at Evelyn, he put the chart down and headed out of the unit to see Caroline.

.Evelyn slowly walking behind him. Her room was partly darkened by the dimmer lights she had asked for. The rooms here were usually bright and painted with the pastels that hospitals favor, bringing a feeling of hope, he guessed. She was sitting up in the bed, a middle-aged woman whose age was so much more obvious now in the absence of the wall of rouge and lipstick and mascara that becomes a fortress against time for them. The surgery had actually gone quite well and he felt confident that the fever was not a warning of a more ominous path.

Inside, he knew that the burden he was now carrying should not interfere with what he must do as a professional, as a doctor whose very presence of personality is part of his armentarium.

"Good afternoon, Caroline." He quietly but solidly said. She looked up at him with weary but not angry eyes.

"Good afternoon, Dr. Martin. I, missed your smiling face this morning. I hope all is well with you."

Frank was a bit stunned by that question. Did she know what was going on? C'mon, Frank, ol' man, do not be so damn paranoid. Just an innocent question. Stop this shit. Answer her.

"Yes, I had an urgent matter that had to be taken care of this morning. But all's well. That is not the question, my dear young lady, the question is how are you?"

"Well, besides the obvious chest pain, a little weary, I must say,"

"Well, you're running a bit of a fever. There were white cells in the urine sample you gave."

Turning to Evelyn, he asked her if a urine culture had been obtained.

"Yes, of course, Dr. Martin" she answered in her usual stem but not impolite manner. "Well, then, does it bum when you pee?" he nonchalantly asked Carol y n without any hint of embarrassment."

"Funny you should ask that. Yes,"

"I am assuming you may well have a urinary tract infection, sweetheart. That is a piece of cake for a great doctor like me to cure here and now."

He enjoyed saying that. It was part of the medical life that he still loved. The really personable stuff. He loved the mechanics of surgery, too, of course, but this was on a different and satisfying plane. A fleeting thought of not doing this again suddenly entered his consciousness but he dismissed it as soon as he could.

She smiled at him, almost flirty he thought. In fact, women responded to him in a warm and mildly erotic fashion.

In fact, Evelyn herself had told him he was not only a terrific cardiac surgeon but a terrific -looking man. That he found quite embarrassing at the time but obviously it was flattering.

"I know that, Dr. Martin." His patient smiled coyly in response. He always seemed to feel that underlying sexual tension with female patients but he had never crossed the line. Never. "So cure me"

Frank managed a mild laugh at that with Evelyn in what seemed like the placebo of mirth. It does work, he thought. "Coming right up"

He ordered another urine culture but started an appropriate course of antibiotics at the same time. Everything else seemed to check out satisfactorily and he reassured her about that.

The rest of his afternoon rounding went well. There were two other patients, both progressing to his satisfaction. Still, no further mention of Ken but he knew it would come sometime. Probably today yet. Well, let it happen. I've got to face this he continued to tell himself. He made the conscious decision, reluctantly, haltingly, to go the doctor's lounge. He did not have to but somehow he knew he must. The elevator ride to the first floor itself was uneventful. Only visitors, faces turned away, staring at the numbers of the floors as it descended. He waited in the rear until everyone had exited.

The lounge was located at the end of a corridor that was lined with photographs of all the men who had preceded him and made their mark in some way or the other. Would his ever be placed next to theirs? They all seemed to have a smile of satisfaction as if their accomplishments would in fact live on forever. This guilt feeling continued to drift over him like a dark cloud stuck in a stationery front. Opening the door into an area so familiar should have been simply a routine matter, accompanied by a neutral emotional state. But this time it wasn't. His breathing was more shallow, his hands slightly cool and wet, the knocking of his heart palpably apparent. Inside were e two of his colleagues, both chatting on a sofa that was part of the furniture, slightly worn now but still a post of camaraderie here at this place On one end was Harry Kahn. A urological surgeon by trade, he was one of the most dapper physicians on the staff. Tall and compact, he radiated the glow of a Hollywood star, handsome and self-confident. But smart as hell. Frank always wondered why he chose urology. No offense, he once told him, but he seemed best fit to be in a setting where his natural wit and charm would be dazzlingly, say just old fashioned family practice or internal medicine. No, Harry said, he liked what he was dong just fine. Next to him was Joseph Wicker. He was the chief of Endocrinology. Nearing seventy, he was set to retire soon but that was a function of the rules of the hospital that required retirement from academia at age seventy. No others could be seen which settled Frank a bit as these two were, well, an appropriate foil for his needs at this time. The need for, well, confrontation with reality.

The lounge was newly painted and the odor, not totally unpleasant still lingered. Three windows were opposite the couch which, at this time of day let the sunshine stream in and cover the walls with dancing shadows. A pleasant scene that calmed Frank a bit. A welcomed respite.

Wicker stopped his conversation and turned to Frank.'

"Well, hello, Frank, Good to see you. I don't usually see you in this lounge at this time of day."

"No. not usually. But this… these are not usual times."

He was not certain that either of them had yet heard but Wicker's face told him he had. "Frank" Wicker started with some hesitation, "I… heard about Ken Laser. A bunch of crap. I heard the guy was a gem in the making. What the hell happened?"

Frank had to decide if he wanted to go on with this standing near them or pull up a chair

Fucking easy decision, he thought. Why am I agonizing over this? But he reached for a nearby chair and drew it up in front of Wicker and Kahn.

"Jesus, Joe. I am really trying to digest this. You probably know about our suit?'

Wicker did not hesitate to answer. If nothing else, he was always direct but very honest and thoughtful

"Yes, I have. I know you lost. But, do you think that was the reason Ken… killed himself?"

"I don't know. He took it very hard." "I guess" Wicker inserted "Frank, I think I've heard" Kahn broke in "that part of your defense was that… Ken was, well, how do I put it, more responsible for any wrongdoing than you were." Frank paused. He again felt his pulse quickening, perspiration in his hands, a feeling of dread that was both unwelcome and foreign.

"Harry, I'm not sure how to answer you. I thought there was no wrongdoing on either of our parts. Really. You know as well as I do that so much of what happens in surgery and in medicine as a whole that is called 'malpractice' or negligence' is really just a bad or unexpected outcome, an act of nature if you will. I don't want to go in detail what took place at that hearing but it did focus on the last minutes of the procedure."

"You know," Wicker inserted himself again. "I have talked about that stuff to my fellows on more than one occasion. Obviously, we don't run into as much crap as you surgical types do but it happens. So, I guess every once and a while I think about that part of medicine. You hear so many horror tales that it makes it sound as if there is a vendetta by the world to 'get doctors. Personally, I do not really believe that. Think about it. Do we do our jobs the way they should be done because that's the way it should be done or do we always keep in mind the possibility that someone out there is ready to sue us? Does it help us or hurt us to be 'policed' in that way? I do not really know the answer'

He sat back in the sofa, seemingly relieved and perplexed a the same time, saying no more than that.,

"Well Joe "Kahn finally responded, a look of very serious intent that Frank had often noticed in him." then we can talk about the role of lawyers and the law in all of this. You know, I've met a few who were real assholes and obviously were using the system to make bucks, big bucks, and have not helped alleviate the feeling of persecution that a lot of docs feel. I think more are honest but I just don't really know the exact numbers. Does it make me practice so-called defensive medicine? I don't know. I don't think I do things with the worry of a malpractice suit hanging over me. At least I don't think about it consciously, maybe subconsciously and all that psychological stuff. Ireally don't think I do. What about you Frank?"

Frank was hoping the conversation would have continued on the question of Ken's death but it had careened off on this tangent of the medical-legal landscape., Well, all right... Let's see where this takes me, he thought.

"Obviously, until all of this, I thought about it some but I don't think it influenced what my final decision I made. At least consciously like you said Harry."

"Well, all right. Frank, the tension here is obviously why would this affect Ken like it did? We know that a lot, maybe most, surgeons sooner or later will be involved in a malpractice suit, frivolous or not. And, God, I don't remember hearing of any doctor killing themselves over one."

"There must have been something else going on with him, don't you think Frank? I mean, had you ever noticed hints along the way that might have given you some clue?" Kahn asked, leaning forward now, more intense as the conversation progressed.

Frank, more engaged now, pondered that question, trying to drift back over time.

"Well, he was very intense. Somewhat of a perfectionist. Dedicated as hell, though. I... knew this trial stuff really rattled him and his confidence."

"I've heard," Kahn said "that he somehow was not involved in the protective medical legal wall that the hospital has in place."

"Yes. He chose, voluntarily, to be in a special program that did not have those protections."

"Pity."

"Yea, it was certainly that"

"Frank, do you know his parents? Have you heard from them?"

Throughout all of this, Frank had hardily given Ken's family a thought. Another pang of guilt, different but still a feeling of guilt, covered him now, like a dark blanket shutting out the sunshine.

"No, not really, I mean no. I have never met them. I do know he came from Detroit and his father worked on the assembly line, I think at Ford. Can't recall what his mother did. Oh yeh, I think he told me she had done some work cleaning, help the family finances to help send Ken thorough med school."

"Real salt of the earth" Kahn interjected.

Frank reflected on that for a moment. "Yes, I guess you could say that, Harry." "And, Frank, when is the funeral? I assume it will be in Detroit."

Stunned, Frank realized he had not thought about either Ken's parents or his funeral. But he had just heard about this. He felt, once again, the strain of guilt and loss of moorings. Jesus, he thought, why didn't I ask about the funeral? Christ!

"Yes... I assume it will be. I plan to talk to Ken's parents today if I can. They must be totally heartbroken."

A pall of silence settled over the three of them for a moment, as if the shade of a window had been drawn between them and the outside world, closeting each of them in their own private thoughts, His face a stud y of utter seriousness, Wicker was the first to speak.

"You know, we all have kids. Losing your child has got to be one of the toughest things a person can go through."

"And in this way. Yes." Kahn answered.

Frank could only nod in agreement, unable to decide on exactly what more to say, the deepening pallor of guilt still unmovable over him.

"Well, Frank. I certainly hope you get back in gear as soon as you can. Best medicine, you know, if you'll pardon the pun, to get this behind you as best you can. You're just too good of a surgeon and a doctor to have this get in your way. Yes, yes, part of us 'doing business' I know that cliche. It is true, you know. I do not know how the future will handle this problem of accountability and the world of lawyers and the law. Just don't know but don't let this screw you up."

"Thanks, Harry. Appreciate the vote of confidence. I am finding this a bit difficult to deal with but hopefully, 'this too shall pass' as they say." "I'm sure it will"

Doubting that it would indeed pass, Frank arose from his chair and told them he was going to finish his rounds and get in touch with Ken's parents. Probably would try to jump up to Detroit for the funeral if at all possible.

As he went to leave the lounge, one of his fellow cardiac surgeons, George Taylor stopped for a minute as he noticed Frank.

"Frank. Just heard about Ken Laser. A damn shame. Heard it was a probable suicide. Jesus that kid took the trial hard, I must say."

"Yes, he sure did. George. I'm in a bit of a hurry but would love to talk to you about this later."

George looked a him in some disbelief. He had always known Frank to be gregarious and cordial. This quick exit was not like him, as if he was trying to escape the scene of the crime.

Walking the halls quickl y, wishing to avoid further conversation now, he headed for the administrator's office. Knowing there might be some unpleasantness awaiting him there, he nevertheless opened the door forcefully, unsure what to expect, but knowing he needed to find the phone number of Ken's parents. He had the rumbling inside that he should, yes must, talk to them.

An attractive, middle-aged blonde looked up from her desk. Frank recognized her as Helen Kent, the real honcho of this office.

"Dr Martin. Well hello. that sly smile. He was becoming more aware of this attraction he seemed to have for women. His good looks had been a plus or him but now, it seemed irrelevant to anything. "what brings you into this office today?"

Hello, Helen. I'm sure you've heard about Dr. Laser."

Helen's smile slowly disappeared and a look of distress seemed to replace it. "Yes, I have. What a tragedy."

"Definitely. Helen, can I ask you a favor?" Of course. What is it?'

"I need the phone number or some way to contact Dr Laser's parents." "That should be easy. Give me a moment." As he watched her go into some files ; he nervously ;looked about the office. No one else was there. He was hoping he would not have to confront the hospital administrator, although there was nothing really to fear from him but he just wanted to move this thing along.

"Here it is. She scribbled a number on a pad of paper and handed it to him. On it was the name, Samuel Laser.

Taking it and placing it in his pocket, he thanked Helen and again, quickly made an exit to the hallway. Where should he make that call? His office? His home? It would be a very serious call. One that he needed to make and one that had to be performed very carefully. My home. I want to leave this place now with all of its bad vibes for him and go to my sanctuary. My safety valve.

The drive homes that day was mentally uncomfortable. Seemingly oblivious to the surroundings which ordinarily actually gave him serenity, his head seemed like a mixing bowl, uncomfortably processing one and then the other thought, Why hadn't he thought of Ken's parents, and worse, the timing of the funeral? Why did he now feel like such an incompetent doctor? Why wouldn't this feeling of guilt vanish? Would it pass soon? Could he be the surgeon he once was before this tragedy?

Neither Carole nor the children were at home when he arrived. He was grateful for that, given his strange and sullen mood. But the familiar surrounds gave him a modicum of peace, rare it seemed these days. The sun was bright in the sky and lavishly filtered throughout the front room, a feature that was by design with it large and open windows. Taking off his jacket and tie, he felt a welcomed sense of relief. Taking the paper Helen had given him, he sat down at his favorite chair, wide, and soft, and dialed the number. His hand a again felt moist and he again felt the pounding his chest. Unfamiliar signs of anxiety. Common now.

A high pitched feminine voice answered. "Hello." Simple but to Frank it sounded like an exploding bomb.

"Mrs. Laser?" he nervously asked.

"Yes, this is Catherine Laser. Who is this?'

"Mrs. Laser. This is Frank Martin. I'm. calling to express my deepest sympathy. Ken was one of my favorite residents. I was crushed. by what happened." There, he said it. A bit easier than he thought it would be.

The silence that followed, although only a few seconds seemed like an eternity to him. What would her reaction be? Would she just hang up? Scream at him?

"Yes, Dr Martin. I know who you are. Ken spoke very highly of you and found it a privilege to serve under you."

Those words shot through him like an arrow. No hanging up, no screaming. Just praise. Jesus.

"Ken was…" he actually was trying to hold back the tears that her comments had evoked. "Ken was a terrific young man. You… don't know how awful I feel about his death." The thought suddenly stuck him that even those words were appropriate and honest, they seemed oddly out of place telling them to his mother.

Sensing her voice cracking a bit, he listened for her answer. "Thank you, Dr Martin. I am still in a frenzy I guess. I cannot… I don't want to believe Ken is gone And… and… killing himself." Now her voice stopped and the undeniable sounds of grief came next, the soft cry of a mother who had lost her child. But losing him as she had. Not to a terrible disease, not by a horrible accident, but by his own hand. He could not imagine how terrifying that must be to endure

He waited, allowing her natural grief to run its course in this conversation. "Mrs. Laser. I would like to come to the funeral. When is it?"

"Tomorrow. It will be at St Matthew's church We live in Redford, The church is on Beach road. I. do not know the address." "What time tomorrow, Mrs. Laser?"

"1:30"

"Thank you. I will find my way there."

"We will appreciate you're coming, Doctor. I really do. Call me if l can be of any help in getting here. Sam and I will both be looking forward to meeting you. Ken spoke… spoke so highly of you. He always aid he hoped someday he could be as good a surgeon a you are."

Frank could not say a word in response. What was probably one of the highest compliment he could have received seemed no like another arrow through his heart.

"Thank you" was all he could say in response. "Ken was one of my favorites. You do not know how awful I feel. I will see you tomorrow."

Hanging up the phone, feeling anchorless remorseful, he waited until Carole came home... Should he ask her to accompany him or would it be better if he went alone to cleanse himself of these demons. When she walked in, a bit surprised, as if he should not be here at this time but these were not normal 'times' obviously.

"Frank, honey, I'm not used to seeing you home at this hour. How did it go today at the hospital?" She was uneasy asking that question. A question she had asked him dozens of times in the course of a normal month. But now, these were not 'normal times'.

"As well as I could expect, I guess, I ran into Harry Kahn and Joe Wicker in the doctor's lounge. Interesting conversation. Can't say it solved anything but interesting. They reminded me of the funeral. I had not thought about it at all and I felt like shit because I had not. I really did. So, I got Ken's parent's number and called. The funeral is tomorrow in an area of Detroit. I'm going to go honey. I really have to go."

Carole moved over and took him in her arms, tears starting to stream down her cheeks. Watching what was happening to him was difficult to endure. Her strong-willed capable surgeon continuing to melt down.

"I know, I know, honey. I know. Yes, you should go I want to go with you. I really do." Frank held her as tightly s she was holding her. His anchor, his rock in this, the most difficult of times for him. Yes, he did want her o to join him. "I want you to come, Carole. I need you."

150

CHAPTER NINETEEN

I Leaving early, the drive to Redford was without incident. Carole sitting next to him, showering him with glimpses of affection and reassurance, made it more pleasant. He had told both Teri and Tim of where and why they were leaving for Michigan. He was surprised how they had both grasped the effect of all of this on their father and asked if they, too, could go but Carole told them while she would have like that, it was best that just the two of them went. Redford was just northeast of downtown Detroit, a pleasant lower middle class area with clean lawns and small but sturdy appearing homes. He had forgotten to ask Catherine Laser initially the location of the funeral and had called back soon after that first conversation. He had located it on his Map Quest. Turning a corner, he easily found it. White with peeling paint on its exterior, medium sized with the identifying cross atop its small steeple, it was about what Frank had expected to encounter Finding a place to park nearby, they slowly exited the car, locking it, and checking it again that it was locked as he had concerns about Detroit and its environs. C'mon, Frank, he told himself, that is a bit elitist. It was a pleasant day, helping his mood just a bit but that dark cloud never did disappear, as he walked hand in hand with Carol to the church. It was about two blocks away, the neighborhood surprisingly well supplied with full grown trees that were just starting to wane in their Fall coloration.

"Kind of lovely here, honey, don't you think?" Carole carefully asked, "Yes, surprisingly so I guess. Hell of a lot of trees."

"Typical Mid-western look." Carole wanted to maintain the small-talk dialogue for now. She was aware of his tension and guilt.

"Yeh"

They remained silent for the remainder of the walk towards the church. Several others were entering at the same time. Frank wanted desperately to find Ken's parents before the service began. He spotted two people sitting in the front pew seemingly acknowledging the sympathies of the attendees. As he walked towards them, he guessed that she was in her middle fifties, he a bit older. Hair graying and pulled back in a severe manner, she wore little make up, perhaps for this day alone. But it made her look unattractive and plain. Her husband, stout and balding, seemed to tower over her even sitting. What hair he had remaining was still dark brown with just a tinge of gray scattered about. He was the first to look up at Frank, seeming to identify but not recognize him. His eyes were set back, sullen almost, carved into a face of sadness. Why not? Frank thought. Why not,'

"Mr. Laser?" he inquired with as much courage as he could muster, "Yes?"

"My name is Frank Martin Your son worked closely with me. I am a cardiovascular surgeon."

Up closer, Frank noticed some of the familiar facial features of his son.

Sam Laser stood up to meet him. He was taller than he imagined when he was sitting. Bulky with a slightly protruding abdomen, Frank could envisage him as a former football player. His dark eyes, set back in his face, projected a certain melancholy state that seemed to fit the moment.

"Dr. Martin. Yes, yes, Ken talked so much about you. I am so glad to meet you."

He grasped Frank's hand with enough pressure to cause a bit of discomfort.

"Mr Laser. I cannot tell you how sorry I am. I just can't. I… admired Ken so much. He was such a promising young surgeon." Frank mostly believed that but he wanted to assure this man that he had nothing but the highest respect for his son.

"Thank you. Your coming means a lot to both of us."

Turning to his wife, Sam Laser patted her on her shoulder as he interrupted her discussion with another woman.

She too stood up dwarfed by her husband, but rather attractive and looking younger, he thought, than she really was.

"Honey, I want you to meet Dr Martin. You know, Ken talked so much about him."

Catherine Laser. Ken's mother. He had told Frank about her on several occasions, how she had come from a dirt poor family, and had to work very hard just to persuade her family to let her graduate high school. Ken admired his mother's native intelligence, her keen sense of right and wrong, and her utter devotion to him and his father.

She looked a him with longing eyes. Why did her son, the pride of her life, the light of her life, do such a thing? What in the world would have happened to make him do this? They had sacrificed so much to get him where he was, that was never a thought, but such a waste, such a waste.

"Yes, Dr Martin. We spoke yesterday. I_am, glad you could make it here but I wish it was under different circumstances".

"Yes, so am I. Can I introduce my wife, Carole, to both of you?"

Carole stepped forward, extending her hand in a gesture of both introduction and grief truly felt. The obvious agony of Ken's mother made a strange but deep impression on her. Did that trial really lead to this? She asked herself.

I am glad to meet both of you" she said as she extended her hand to them.

'I did not know your son that well but Frank always spoke so highly of him"

He could not recall, in the years ahead, how he felt that moment when Catherine Laser stuck the dagger into his heart.

"Dr Martin, why did you try to make Ken the scapegoat on this?"

Those words froze him in place. All of the guilt, all of the regrets that he was feeling came forth again. The rapid heart beat, the sweaty palms returned, all of the signs that were so foreign to him, signs that reminded him of his humanity and his part in all of this. Unexpected as the question was a that moment, even a bit out of place here and now, he knew that sooner or later he would have to confront the grief of his parents and now, obviously, at least her anger, he was uncertain how to answer.

"I'm not certain what you mean, Mrs, Laser?"

"OH, I'm sure you do."

"Catherine! Please, not now, please" her husband urged as he took her by the arm and tried to silence her.

"Yes, now." She answered as she pulled her arm away from him. "Ken told us how that trial went. It hurt him deeply. It made him feel very guilty and resentful. He cried every time I talked to him when it was over. My son was a good doctor, Dr Martin, and he respected you so much. You betrayed him."

"Please, Dr Martin," Sam Laser began to plead. "she is very upset as you can see a this horrible time of our lives. Ken was our only child and… we were so proud of him and we loved him so."

Frank stood frozen in place. He felt Carole's arm around him as he gathered his thoughts and tried to formulate the words that would satisfy him and her. What words would that be? Why did she do this before the funeral? Had she been harboring all of this anger and simply could not restrain herself?

"You don not know how sorry I am about what happened, Mrs. Laser. Ken was one of my favorites. I am heartbroken!… think what was portrayed at that trial was truthful."

"Mr. and Mrs. Laser," Carole thought she needed to break in "Frank always spoke highly of him. He had been rocked by this, believe me. I know we cannot feel what you are going through. We have two children and I can only imagine. Please accept our deepest sympathy. He so wanted to be here today to show our respect."

Sam Laser look approvingly at her and put his arm around his rather diminutive wife, calming her in a way that appeared to be a familiar gesture with them. Whatever flowed between seemed to be flowing as she drew herself up and let a smile crawl over her face, minimal, but a smile nevertheless with its promise of forgiveness.

"I'm sorry, Mrs. Martin, truly I am" Elizabeth Laser looked forlornly at both of them. "I am. I am so miserable. So damn miserable." With that she stepped forward, quickly taking Carole into her arms, the tears starting to flow now. Carole towered over her but she melted easily into her, seemingly deriving comfort from her presence. Frank was quite relieved, the anxiety slowly diminishing and the tension more tolerable.

En during the service was not easy. It focused on Ken's early life, his devotion to his parents, his hard-working habits, and the total commitment of everyone in his family to insuring his success in medical school and afterwards. Going into the inability to answer the whys of his death, the pastor invoked a number of theological explanations, grasping on the ever reliable God "works in mysterious ways and he was now with his Lord in heaven."

CHAPTER TWENTY

He had wrestled with religion and arrived recently at the conclusion that he really did not care much about it. Raised in a Lutheran family with loose church connections, his parents had not pushed any particular sets of belief on him or on his two younger sisters. But the concept of a supernatural being continued to be, while not a central ingredient of his thinking, not foreign. Lately, the concept had become just that and he seldom attended any church services or consciously attempted to impart any religious doctrines in his children. Carole, while coming from a family with even looser church attendance, drifted a bit more to it than he and frequently took them to church, with no objection from him. Now, here, amidst a flood of religious imagery and strongly held beliefs, he felt a bit alien. While grieving for Ken and aware of his own building guilt about what had happened, he did not feel the need to attempt to expunge himself via any religious rituals. Approaching the Lasers following the ceremony, he continued to feel that uneasiness as if he was a pat of butter ready to be dropped into the fire.'

"Thank you, again, Dr Martin, for coming", Sam Laser offered "will you be joining all of us at the cemetery?"

Wishing to decline, knowing that would most likely increase his feelings of guilt but seeing Carole nodding her assent, he reluctantly agreed.

"Of course we plan on coming. That is the least we can do."

"Yes, certainly" Carole added "we wondered if this would be just family. Will there be a procession?"

"Yes" Sam Laser answered. "Just drive up to the drive of the church and the officer will give you a blue flag to put on your car. Then, well, just join the caravan."

"Of course"

Frank, taking Carole's hand, turned to leave the church, nodding to those residents he recognized.

Finally outside, he turned to Carole, relieved but dreading that next step," well, that went, how should I put it, like a boat on a wave inside a hurricane"

"I guess that is what we should have expected. I think Ken was their only child."

"He never mentioned any siblings and we sure didn't meet any in there. Yes, I know it must be tough. To lose a kid, to lose him by his own hand. Just a crock of shit. Period." They walked silently towards their car, still hand in hand, the cool breezes of Fall swirling about, cooler here than in Chicago, but still refreshing after that crowded church setting. Inside, starting the motor, and moving forward towards the drive they saw a number of other cars with a blue flag attached to their front. Pulling over to a uniformed policeman with a handful of those flags, Frank took one and was told to simply get in line. Doing so, he noticed that there were more cars than he had anticipated. The Lasers were well-known in the area and well-liked and Ken had been a constant presence growing up here. Not surprising then. Next to him, the officer now speeded on his motorcycle to lead the procession to the cemetery. They drove through areas that seemed, to Frank at least, a bit blighted, emptying soon into surprisingly more affluent appearing vistas and finally, into a long drive that led into the cemetery. Flowers adorned many of the gravesites and tall trees seemed to guard all of it, well kept lawns projecting an aura of total serenity. It was obvious where the burial would take place, the hearse stopping by a newly dug grave, the area relatively untouched but surrounded by tall oak trees which spread their shadows over the ground as if to protect that final resting place for eternity. Carole and Frank stepped out of their car and walked up to the area, the gravesite now surrounded by a mass of humanity. In the center, the Lasers and the clergyman. Six men, three of whom were residents from the hospital, carried Ken's coffin up to the platform above the grave. More tributes to Ken and his tragically shortened life woven within the liturgical passages of the Laser's faith and finally, the lowering of the coffin. Tears amply displayed, audible crying clearly expressed all of which again bore into Frank's consciousness. Ken's death, a bit abstract to him at first, now seemed all too real. All of this very surreal, distant, almost like a dream but Frank knew it wasn't. What he did not know was that it would alter his life in ways that even now did not seem possible. When the burial ceremonies were over, Frank and Carole extended their final condolences to the Lasers. Catherine, visibly grief stricken and shaken attempted to again thank them but for whatever reason could not resist one final commentary on all of it.

"But none of this, none of this, would be happening if that damn trial... sorry, Dr, Martin. Thank you again. Ken would have been pleased to know you cared"

Speechless again, Frank merely nodded nondescritly, turned and walked down the path to their car. He would never see the Lasers again.

CHAPTER TWENTY ONE

The ride back to Chicago was rather melancholy. Few words were exchanged between Frank and Carole. Each, perhaps, had their own thoughts. His were filled with a sad mixture of enduring grief, that relentless guilt, and concerns about whether he could ever regain that sense of confidence and purpose that drove him to become what he wanted to be. He just could not shake off that feeling of loss, of not being able to get there again, ever. Hers was concern about his change since all of this began and particularly since Ken's suicide. She too, noticed a tenseness that was foreign, it seemed to his persona. Affectionate he still was but with more of a sense of detachment than she liked and ever felt before. Their frequency of intercourse was less but even more, less intense and abandoned. Hopefully, she mused, this too shall pass.

"That was a bit difficult for me, Carole" he had finally told her. "I find it a challenge to understand the reasons for what Ken did. Surely, it was not just the result of that trial, although the Lasers, or at least, Catherine, thinks it was."

Watching the passing traffic, looking at the never ending expanse of farmland that now surrounded them, Carole had felt as if she was in a bit of a trance, daydreaming, perhaps, but his words jolted her back to realty.

"It was all so sad, honey. I know how this is eating you up. But we, you, have to get through this and back to being that wonderful, competent, admired surgeon that you are."

He reached over and took her hand and gripped it tightly, a wan smile now, new, thank God, she thought, at least he is inching his way back to that former Frank that offered so much to so many.

Thinking their own thoughts, the rays of sun filtering through the windows, promising, perhaps, a new day and new hope. This was getting so philosophical, she thought now. Let's just get back to the old way. Finally, the houses of the Chicago suburbs began their parade, replacing the waves of farmland as civilization's face changed. Entering the familiar stretch of their street and finally their driveway, Carole hoped that this ordeal could now become part of their history, past, not forgotten, but not the present.

Not feeling up to the challenge of cooking that evening, having arrived just after Tim and Teri had finished their school day, they decided to go out for a nice Italian dinner, that being Teri's favorite, and a real treat on a school night. Surprisingly very little was asked or said about that morning and the funeral as they prepared to leave together for the trip to Antonio's, their favorite family Italian eatery, perhaps a ten mile drive. Whether being together like that or just the familiar sights of their neighborhood, Frank felt a bit more serene and began to ask each of his children about their school day. This was a frequent exercise, feeling that it showed his interest, a genuine one, in their schooling and his way of bonding.

"We are studying the Revolution and the Constitution, Dad" Tim began. "I like it. I really do dig American history for some reason"

"No reason needed, Tim. American history is interesting and important. I minored in that in college before I went into Medical School. Might have ended up being a history professor."

"Really?" Tim asked incredulously

"Really"

"It is true, Tim" Carole chimed in, so happy to see some semblance of family normalcy after that gloomy morning. "Your dad was a whiz in history. Actually, he was a whiz in about every subject t he took."

Frank smiled, taking solace in her words of praise. But it was true. He was a straight A student and found his pre med college life extraordinarily satisfying. He had met Carole in his senior year of high school and they had carried on their relationship at college. There she was a business major, president of her sorority, and active in campus political life. Dynamic and beautiful, their relationship continued. He was quite handsome, of course, and she had discovered quickly the level of his intelligence. Her sorority sisters could not praise him enough, as he had dated one or two of them with Carole's permission, and was considered a 'real catch'. When he was accepted to medical school on the East Coast, she had decided to go for an MBA and would try to gain admission at the same school, prestigious as it was. Frank never doubted she would be accepted, her intelligence and drive standing out in the crowd, her grades teeming with mostly A's. Screaming with delight when the acceptance came, she was as thrilled to be able to continue to share his life as she was to gain acceptance to one of the top business schools in the county. Hopelessly in love, they both decided marrying was the reasonable approach for both of them but they would take every precaution to avoid pregnancy until she at least completed the two years of her MBA curriculum.

Their wedding took place in Rockford, a middle-sized city just west of Chicago. They had both grown up there and had substantial roots with both of their families still living rather close by. Their parents were very cordial to one another and quite pleased with the union of the high school beauty queen and its star male athlete and student, the valedictorian who was so damn handsome according to her mother. They both excelled in their graduate schools as they had in undergrad. She rose quickly towards the top of her class and he was, as always, blessed with those infernal A's as she called them. Finishing medical school at the top of his class, he had no problem obtaining a surgical residency and subsequent cardiac specialization fellowship at the medical center associated with his school. She had obtained an excellent position with a large advertising firm and wanted to stay put until he finished his training and they could either return to Illinois or make another decision. Physically attracted to one another as well as emotionally, they seemed to find enough time and then some for sex even with his busy schedule during that arduous period of training. At the end of that four year post-graduate grind, he felt he was a s capable as any fellow who had matriculated they decided to return to the Midwest and looked specifically to Chicago and its environs, both to be closer to their parents and because they both liked the city and he knew that area could obviously support another cardiovascular surgeon. And so it went. Two children later, an era that now seemed centuries ago to Carole. She had found a position in a marketing firm in downtown Chicago, rising rapidly up the ladder until she hit the 'glass ceiling' But she had decided to be a mother first and keep her career on hold, resigning to raise Tim and Teri while Frank advanced to become one of the highest regarded cardiovascular surgeons in the city. And now.

The restaurant was bright and cheery, with prints of paintings depicting the usual, familiar sights of Italy, checkered tablecloths with the ubiquitous bottle of olive oil sitting squarely in the middle. Frank thought some wine would be not only appropriate to the setting but to his basic psychological state of the moment. Carole agreed and they ordered a bottle of the restaurant's best Chianti. There is something soothing about sitting down in a restaurant engulfed by one's family, waiting to share the pleasures of food and light conversation. Both Frank and Carole hoped this would happen tonight, bringing the simple rewards of life to offset the horrors. So they each ordered in turn, Tim his favorite pasta, Teri her ravioli, and Frank and Carole variations of veal.

"Now, Dad" Tim began "tell us how it went this morning. Were there a lot of people?"

"Yes, quite a few" he warily replied. How much do I tell them? Just the outlines? How I really feel?

So he outlined their trip, the meeting with Ken's parents, the service, the burial, the tears, the emotions of everyone except his.

With the aid of two glasses of the Chianti and the never disappointing taste of Antoni's veal, he became more philosophical and his mood less dark.

"So, Dad, Teri had asked:" it's back to the grind for you, huh? I'm glad this is over, even though I feel bad for what happened to Dr. Laser."

Carole took it upon herself, now, to answer that question. "Yes, honey. It's back to the grind again. But it isn't a grind for your Dad. Really. He loves what he is doing and he is very, very good at it. Both of you should be as lucky as he. Doing something you truly love and be so darn good that you never want to do anything else."

Relaxed now, sitting in this place, Frank savored those words, let them marinate through his brain, hoping they would be the therapy he needed. But oh that that would indeed be the case!

CHAPTER TWENTY TWO

Frank eased back into what he hoped would be 'the routine' challenging by any measurement, a cardiovascular surgeon's 'routine' is anything but routine. Noticing a slight drop-off in his usual numbers of consultations, he remained unfazed by that. But he found it more difficult than he thought was possible returning to the operating room with the confidence he had always displayed. Haunted by the memory of Ken he simply was not able to be as effective as he thought he needed to be not to put his patients in jeopardy.

"Frank, honey" Carole told him when he discussed it with her "maybe we should just take a long vacation until you work this out as I' am sure you will. You are just too good a doctor to feel like this. Maybe, maybe you... you could see someone?"

Sensing her concern and bewildered by how all of this had affected him, he pondered whether to see a psychiatrist. While he still was aware of the connotation that carried, it was less of a problem in today's world but he did not think he was ready to make that move yet. A long vacation? How could he take off more time, having devoted enough to the trial and its tragic consequences? Well, maybe. But, all right, he felt he could benefit from, if nothing else, a

167

week somewhere completely removed, or at lest, somewhat removed from civilization, "You probably are right, dear. Tell you what let's go to that island we were once at, you know, whatever its name, sitting tucked away in the Caribbean with no amenities except sun, sand and good food."

Carole, surprised but pleased, slid back in time to when they visited that island, remote but planted in the middle of that vast blue sea that was known s the Caribbean. It was one of the best weeks they had ever spent together, just before she became pregnant with Tim.

Oh, great, honey" she responded jubilantly" I know it will do you good. Everything has been so serious, so serious and… Listen, I'll get Mom and Dad to drive down here to take care of the kids. They love to do that, you know."

Now filled with something that had been quite foreign to him over these past few months, hope, he readily agreed and with the energy that had been diluted now arose again as he made the appropriate changes in his schedule and enlisting the help of his colleagues for coverage for the week.

Leaving early on a Saturday morning, the drive to 0'Hare seemed almost melancholy, as if he was leaving a concrete chip that had weighed him down these past several months. It felt exhilarating, this drive, the trees now bare of their leaves, the air cool and warning of the coming winter. In contrast to previous absences from home, both Tim and Teri welcomed their departure. Both had sensed the change in their father's disposition, his lack of levity and response that they had come to expect and love. Both hoped wherever they were going would help him forget all of this and make him like he was. Carole's parents, still quite active in their early 70's, had been well aware of what had unfolded and agreed with their daughter that this may be just what the doctor ordered, so to speak. Henry, her father, was tall but still lean and athletic.

Retiring from his auto dealership five years ago, he was very active in doing "those things he always wanted to do": golf, gardening and traveling. Not a bad life, Frank had told him, although at the time not even remotely considering retiring from what he did. Her mother Helen, still a strikingly attractive woman at 70 was as personable as she was intelligent, qualities that, to him, obviously passed through to his wife, including her beauty. Their frequent visits here were welcomed, playing a role in forming strong bonds with his children. Leaving them that morning seemed easier than in the past, reflecting, he postulated the expectations of relaxation and possible exorcism of those demons.

"You happy about this, honey?" Carole asked as they neared O'Hare

"Totally. For the first time in months, I actually feel relaxed. Maybe I can get the visions of Ken out of my mind"

She reached over to touch his arm, a gentle sign of her devotion and her determination to chaperone the exorcism in anyway she could. Even sexually.

They used a valet service, as they had in the past, and arriving at O'Hare he even rejoiced in the mass of humanity that typified the place, sharing their desire to be off and running to wherever for whatever purpose. Weaving their way through the oceans of people, they arrived at the gate bearing the name of their destination. Even seeing the simple words posted in front of them added to the swirling current of hope Frank was experiencing. Boarding the plane, he glanced about to see who else was going to share in the exultation of entering such a totally different environment than Chicago. Young people, some even dressed now in shorts with the expectation of soothing warmth, elderly couples, affluent enough to leave whenever they wanted he guessed, others who formed a mini-melting pot on this steel and aluminum flying bird he was about to enter. He had decided to treat himself to first class seats, not to demonstrate any elitism, but simply because he wanted the comfort on this trip and he could afford it. Seating themselves in the wider, softer seats did bring more of a sense of pleasure befitting the importance of this 'get-away' As the plane pulled way from the terminal, joining a long line of other steel and aluminum birds, all with different but important destinations, he eagerly took in all of his surrounding, as if this was his ultimate escape. Stopping just for a moment, the engines on the birds began revving up to its full potential and like a arrow shot from a bow, began its accelerating run down the cement path and then that breathtaking moment when it left the confines of the earth and ascended towards the vast, never-ending skies.

He sat next to the window, which he always preferred, to enjoy the rapture of abandoning one's bolting to earth's gravity to view the spectacle from far above. He watched as the tall bricked skyscrapers of Chicago's loop slowly gave way to the endless carpet of suburbs and then the solitude of the prairie below. His reveries were briefly interrupted by the stewardess asking him if he wished anything to drink.

"Uh, yes," he answered, "bring me some orange juice and vodka.

He ordinarily did not drink much in the way of alcohol this early in the day but he enjoyed its mind easing effect and the opportunity to contemplate on a whole range of things here in the air with nowhere else to go.

Carole had moved her hand to his and they clenched each other tightly as he looked approvingly at her smile

"This is just what we needed, Honey" she said again. Was she trying to reassure herself that this would be the circumstances that would sooth him, solve his dilemma, ease him back to the level that she wanted him to once again reach She only hoped. He was too young and talented to waste it.

Looking over to her, Frank tried to reassure her as much as he was trying to reassure himself:" I'm sure it is. And, taking his newly delivered orange juice and vodka inside the plastic cup towards her "I'11 drink to that"

Unexpectedly, perhaps, she leaned over and gave him a stolen touch of her lips on his cheek. "'Thanks, I needed that" he gleefully responded, sipping the enticing mixture and feeling an immediate sense of well-being. Maybe it will do it, he thought. Drive those fucking demons away for good. He leaned back in the cushioned chair, enjoying the fleeing clouds below and continuing to gain some balance with the help of the vodka. The flight moved along effortlessly, encountering only a few bumps here and there to interrupt his musings. Before long, having read a bit and enjoying a second drink, the announcement came that they were preparing their final descent into the magical island of St. Vincent.

At first just a dot on the vast sheet of water below, it rapidly grew larger with the planes final approach and the pilot, to Frank's relief, landed the big bird on the rather small runway for this rather small island. But he could feel the magic already. Relief was here; a cure may be in hand, open the doors and let him escape the shrouds of Chicago.

CHAPTER TWENTY THREE

St Vincent's was everything Frank and Carole remembered from their visit there before their children were born, Tucked into the waves of the Caribbean, it was small enough to offer anonymity but big enough to give succor. Frank always marveled at the calming effect of the ocean, not just water, but the ocean. Maybe it was the rhythm of the waves pounding against the beach, maybe the palm trees that guarded the majesty of the land against the sea, may be the endless cloudless days of the islands that populated these oceans. The hotel in which they stayed was the newest on the island, brimming with tropical themes, their room spacious and opening unto the nearby beach with the ocean's never-ending slap encouraging the kind of sex that Frank had not remembered for several years. It was unencumbered by the presence of their children in nearby rooms, the constant threat of his being interrupted by a call from either a patient or the hospital, or the need to be precise in the timing

It started almost from the first moment they were escorted into their room by a friendly thin porter with that island accent that he always found charming and cheerful. The day was spectacular, the sun unguarded by any clouds, the sands of the beach, visible from their room, glistening, the ocean beckoning, "Honey" she had said, "let's get into our bathing stuff and go out to that beach. I know how you love it,"

"And I do" he had had answered "I'm with you on that"

Not putting away any of their other clothes, she found their swimming gear right on top of the suitcase. Deciding to undress here and now, Carole removed her blouse and skirt, now only in her bra and panties. She of course, was gorgeous, with a figure that was stunning in any degree of dress or undress. Undoing her bra revealed her ample breasts and as she slid her panties off, the nakedness of her body in this setting, at this time, was almost too much for him to resist. Sensing that, she moved towards him and wrapping her arms around his neck, kissed him passionately. The touch of her naked body aroused him quickly and she aided him as he too flew out of his clothes, Her hand grasped his penis which was in full erection even now and their passion enveloped them in a curtain of love and eroticism, just as she hoped, this trip would provide. They engaged in varieties of sex that they had not experienced in a long time, too long Frank thought. She didn't hesitate to offer oral sex which he returned in kind. It culminated in an orgasmic eruption that seemed to drain the last ounce of anxiety out of him. He lay back in the bed, perspiring in the tropical heat even with the air conditioning in the room churning away, relaxed and at, last happy.

Carole hugged him closely, her body as soaked and yet unclear of the lotions of love.

"Umm, you big hunk, you" she teased him" kissing him repeatedly on his cheek." That, my dear handsome husband, was one hell of a fuck I must say"

He responded with the sort of wistfulness that characterizes our youth, flippant but pleased, feeling that the best is yet to come.

"Agree. But you were no wall-flower either. Never seen you use your mouth as well as you did."

"Pu-lease, dear. You know I have no problem with sucking that big cock of yours"

She didn't talk like that very much, actually, and she felt uncertain if that was what she really needed to say but she wanted to raise the erotic bar as high as she could over this few days of their grand get-away.

And so it went for the next five days. Sex every night, sleeping in until almost 10:00, a rare treat for any surgeon, but so welcomed after those agonizing months of darkness and guilt, sitting on the golden sand with the water lapping their feet, strolling along the beach, hand in hand, he noting the frequent glances of the other men towards his wife, stunning in her bikini suit with her hair flowing over her shoulders. He drank more than he normally would allow himself, sampling those exotically named concoctions that promised more than they delivered but were fun, he thought. Carole, who was a wine devotee, decided to join him on occasion, agreeing that they were more fun than what a true connoisseur of alcohol would recommend.

It was the night of their last day. Tanned and content, they had spent the day doing just about what they expected to do, not very much. Late in arising, they had stayed in bed again and embraced in a tangle of trust and love that had fortified Frank's disposition. He thought, indeed, those demons that had hovered around had been chased. But he still had the uneasy feeling that they were not completely vanquished. She dressed in her swimsuit with an accompanying robe appropriate for the setting and he had thrown on some long shorts lying beneath a tee shirt emblazoned with the St Vincent's logo. While her beauty was a given, she had always admired his strikingly handsome visage coupled with a body well in shape for a man who had such little time to devote to conditioning.

"Well, sweetie" he addressed her as they faced each other in these island garbs, admiring each other's bodies. "Off to the luscious spread of eggs, toast, waffles, and rolls. And more too."

"Coffee, coffee, coffee, my gallant St Vincennite. Coffee! A fair Miss must have her coffee to face such a hard day's work ahead. I mean how can anyone sit out hat beach, walk along the water, and sleep with no fuel? You tell me."

"Can't. Off to the filling station" he replied with a merriment that seemed so different than he had felt. This was truly paradise.

Breakfasts at this resort was a cornucopia. Bowels of fresh fruit surrounded a display of pastries covered with blueberries strawberries and cheese. There were chocolate doughnuts, glazed doughnuts, plain donuts, and cinnamon twists stacked high. On another table, the aroma of cooking eggs with slabs of bacon, mountains of butter. You could step across the room where a smiling native would gladly cook an omelet to order or prepare a Belgian waffle with pecans or fruit and gallons of syrup if desired. Frank had never quite seen a display like this and the temptation to indulge was overwhelming and he loaded his plate higher than he wished Carole ate less but with equal vigor and appreciation of this wondrous offering. Sitting by a table adjacent to the open veranda, the sea breezes floated about them, the gentle sound of the waves adding a symphony of the tropics that was too sensuous for anyone not to wish to keep forever. A short stout waiter came by, asking them with that accent that always enchants if they wished some coffee.

"You bet." He said "Let it flow"

Smiling, the waiter filled their cups with black, steaming coffee. Indigenous to this island the coffee was sensational and Frank drank cup after cup, daring his heart to speed up in objection. It never did.

They finished their breakfast in a leisured manner, intermittently mingling bites of food, drinks of the heavenly coffee, and enjoying the sight and sounds of the nearby ocean. Smiling in unison as the waiter bade them a pleasant day, they strolled out of the dining area, now filled with a spectrum of older couples, the grayness of their hair outlined by the evolving tanning of their faces, younger couples, some with their children and the occasional lone figure, perhaps seeking to find love and sex sometime during this trip, or so they surmised.

Spying them, a youngish looking teen-ager ran over, his slim body tanned to a golden hue, his white teeth shining through like a light bulb.

"Sir! May I help you once more today? I will get you the most desirable spot on this beach."

Mureto was his name, they had learned. He had just finished high school and was uncertain of his future but during this season decided tow work as a beach boy, both for the money and the chance to be on the beach, which he enjoyed immensely Personable and efficient, they had grown fond of him in just a matter of a few days. But he did manage to tie down some of the better areas on the rather crowded beach, erecting a huge umbrella that spread its shadow over them and much more. With the gesture of a generous tip, gladly received by the young man, they settled in on the two beach chairs Meurto had provided, hands held, eyes partly closed, hearing that inexorable rush of water on the sand. Frank drifted off into half slumber, his mind now quiet and, seemingly at peace with the world, for the first time in many days, the shadow of Ken gone. Carole looked a him, smiled, and lay back in reverie. Would her hero conquer this sudden intrusion on their life? Could he return to the world as she knew it, his marked capabilities highlighted by an admirable layer of compassion that truly made him one of the best surgeons in the entire big ol city of Chicago? Could he? Oh, God, let him. Let him.

It was over much sooner than either one of them wished. Prompting Frank to consider extending their stay. But, the scheduling was already completed and he did not wish to disrupt it any more than was necessary. It had been a wonderful few days of total r relaxation mixed with that dose of daily sex that gave them both immeasurable pleasure and bonding. He had told her that he thought he was ready to face the world again with, he hoped, a much better outlook. As their plane ascended back into the endless blue, Carole braced herself for what she knew would be an incredibly important time in their lives.

Chapter Twenty Four

Meloncholy. Frank thought of the return flight as a symbiosis of joy and dread. He turned quickly to the window as the plane ascended into the blue skies and started to head North. That magnificent island, first a broad expanse of palm trees and sand dissolved quickly into but a dot in the middle of the vast darkness of the ocean. He had hoped he had collected himself, programmed all of what had been and what, hopefully, would be into an acceptable compromise with the demons of the past year. Exorcise? Not likely. Compromise? Hopefully. Carole turned to him, reached for his hand, held it tightly, smiled enough as she turned to her and was met with that oh so beautiful visage that had always enchanted him.

"Penny for your thoughts, darling? She softly asked.

Hesitating for just a moment, the answer was, partly the truth, partly a daring sense of manufactured optimism.

"It was a hell of a time. Really. And you, my gorgeous and so faithful wife had a lot to do with that, in many many ways. I think it has help me get the world in some degree of order, at lest as I once knew it. I am looking forward to returning to the old routine of saving lives."

"Oh, Frank, I was so hoping I would hear that kind of attitude. My ol' guy is back!" she squeezed his hand firmly, hoping to transmit her flow of optimism to him.

A river of thoughts accompanied by a sea of emotions accompanied him back on that flight. Yes, he was looking forward to the return to his previous life, his practice with all of its challenges and rewards. But would he be able to pick up where he left off before all of this began? Could he, did he, get over that black cloud that hung over him. He felt he had but he just wasn't certain.

Clouds hung over Chicago and the rest of the Mid-west as the plane approached O'Hare, revealing bits and pieces of the brown landscape below reflecting the onset of winter, the trees denuded of their bright foliage now. Awaiting the arrival of the inevitable blankets of snow. Noticing a slight loss of the sunny optimism absorbed from the tropical ambience he had just left, he tried to dismiss that threatening return of the black cloud.

Breaking his reverie, Carole signaled their approach and their arrival back home. She was a bit eager to see the children again, still in that arena of parenthood in which young children still dominare, to some extent, one's life.

"Doesn't quite look like the ol'island, does it?" he asked longingly. "No, not quite" she quietly laughed in return "but it's home"
"And so it is, and so it is"

The voice of the attendant formally announced their arrival: "Ladies and Gentleman, welcome to Chicago's O'Hare field where the time is 3:30 Central. If you are catching another plane, please consult the boards in the terminal for the gate. If this is your final destination, we hope you have enjoyed your wonderful time in St. Vincent's and welcome home. Your luggage will be found on carousel eight"

And so they descended the plane through the jet way and into the melee, once again, of the guts of O'Hare, squirming through the mass of humanity once more to retrieve their luggage and head back home and start again.

Driving through the familiar pathways of Chicago as they jostled with their fellow commuters in the thick of rush hour, Frank reminisced again on then week that just passed. He knew it could never be duplicated. The never ending sun with its healing warmth, the plush trees, the beautiful sandy beaches and the melodic rhythm of the ocean's waves, the great food, and, and the sex. God the sex. That was worth the trip itself. Finally pulling into their driveway, he had the sensation that they had never been away. Funny how that feels. Familiar scenes breed familiar feelings and make recent unassociated events now just a distant memory. Funny how that worked. No sooner had the car made its final approach, the front door opened and both Tim and Teri darted out from the door, eager to greet their parents, old enough to fend a bit for themselves but still hovering in that interface between childhood and adolescence.

Mommy, Daddy" Teri screamed, unshackling her joy in that innocence still possessed by the young.

"How was it?" Tim immediately followed eager to know what an island in the Caribbean might be like.

"Terrific, kids, just terrific 1/Carole answered she hugged them both. "We'll tell you and Grandma and Grandpa all about it after we get ourselves a bit settled, OK?"

Tim helped his father lift their luggage out the trunk and carrying it into the house, all were met by Carole's parents, just as eager to hear about their tropical adventure and if, if, it had been a panacea for the terrible times of the past few months. Carting the luggage into the bedroom, the six of them sat down in the living room with its wide open full length windows allowing the remnants of the afternoon sun to shower the area with enough radiance to simulate all seasons.

Carole and Frank went over in detail their adventure in Paradise. Teri interrupted them frequently with question after question, fascinated by the details of a little island 'stuck all by itself out there' and the fun it would be to frolic in the sand and wade into the ocean. Carole's father, gourmet diner that he was, couldn't get enough of the quality and quantity of the food they consumed. Obviously, no mention was made or consideration given to what they did at night, other than admiring the brightness of the moon"

"Well", Lillian decided to finally end the conversation, "I have made some of the best, best food you could find north of the island of St Vincent's. Frank, penne pasta tossed with marinated shrimp. Yum, Yum?"

Yum yum, indeed, Lii. You sure know how to get to a son-in-law's heart" His relationship with Carole's parents had, over the years, evolved into one of mutual respect. Solid people, religious in name only but with wonderful spiritual values. They admired him, both as a husband and as a father, but as a very accomplished surgeon.

"Yum Yum for me, too" Teri chimed in, a granddaughter that Lillian and Roger were so proud of. As a matter of fact, they felt their daughter was very lucky to have the situation she did.

"Well, of course, my little gourmet diner. Didn't grandma give you a whole bunch of yum yum stuff while your Mom and Dad were away?"

"The best, grandma, the best"

Frank was bathing in all of this good cheer and family solidarity. It seemed to cement the week he had just spent, beckoning him to climb out from under the black cloud. But he still could not seem to do it.

Sitting down, starting to inch into the dinner, the salad of nature's best colors, still wet with the dressing, the fresh bread, firm and hot with the thick crust that Frank loved, and then the pasta, flavored as only his Mother -in-law could flavor it, it was truly a trophy of culinary ingenuity.

"Frank." Roger finally asked" when will you return to your practice again?"

"Tomorrow, Roger. I think I'm ready to do my thing." He wanted to say that with a true sense of conviction but he just could not do it, the absence of total conviction arousing the discomfort of underlying anxiety.

Once again, he slept fitfully. While no surgery was on tap, he would go into the office and see patients scheduled for consultation. Would they all show? Would his flow of patients dry up after all that had transpired? So far, he had not really noticed but the threat still seemed real to him. And so came the a morning, rays of sunshine creeping into his room, the alarm waiting to signal the start of the day but he had been awake for what seemed hours already. Turning off the switch to the alarm, he arose out trying to disturb Carole but she too must not have rested well as she turned to him.

"Good morning, darling" she spoke with the cadence of one who is still half asleep. "Morning, baby. I was hoping not to awaken you."
"Too late, already there. I know you are a bit anxious, Frank, but everything will be just fine, believe me."

"I do, hon. I'm fine."

"Let me fix you some breakfast."

"You know, that sounds good. I don't really feel like tramping into the hospital cafeteria today. How about some eggs and a bagel and gobs of that great Starbucks coffee you brew?"

"My pleasure. I'll join you. The kids won't be up for an hour so we'll just continue out little vacation one more day."

And so they did. Frank managed to enjoy the scrambled eggs and the cinnamon-raisin bagels he liked so much and could not get on St Vincent's. And the coffee. While it was good there, nothing was like a good hot cup of extra bold Starbucks and he swabbed down two full cups, enjoying every drop. Carole joined him across the table, savoring the bagels and the coffee.

"Frank" she addressed him as she reached across the table to grasp his hand, "it was truly a magnificent week. I want to tell you that I enjoyed all of it, especially the sex."

Looking at her somewhat quizzically, he wasn't certain why she threw that in. Was he especially proficient with her? Was that her way of encouraging him to face the battles ahead? Or did he just downright enjoy it for its own sake? And, did it make any difference? Probably not. She was his anchor and he did not want to disappoint her.

"Well, my love. That is certainly one of the nicest compliments a man can receive"

And so, they finished their breakfast together, basking in the love they shared. She gave him a prolonged start ut passionate embrace as he climbed into his car and waved good-bye as he prepared to, maybe, start all over again. That drive, that familiar drive with its snapshots of the Lake and the magnificent landscaping continued to enthrall him, especially today. He grew more confident as he approached the doctor's parking lot, pulled in, took a deep breath and dedicated himself to making the past just that, the past. As he exited his car, a familiar voice called out to him.

"Jesus, Frank! Where in the hell have you been?"

Turning to his left, his eyes met those of Gary Carson. One of his favorites even though he came on quite strongly in his approach to medicine and life.

"Gary, my man" he put his arm around his friend in a sincere acknowledgement of their relationship. "Well, to be honest, I took Carole away from it all and flew down to a neat little hiding place at St Vincent's.

"Yeh I have to be honest. Never been there but I bet it was terrific. You needed that, buddy, with all that shit that's happened. Ken and all. But, good to see you. This ol' hospital needs its best cardiac guy back."

"Thanks, Gary, l needed that." He answered with as much humor and play on words as his mood would allow.

They proceeded into the hospital entrance, its large revolving door inviting Frank back into it's womb, which, he hoped would be as warm and comfortable as it was pre-trial. Several of their colleagues passed them by, nodding to him with a sign of welcome and even words of encouragement. So far, so good.

"No cutting today?" Gary inquired as they neared the elevator.

"No, not today. Office stuff, getting back in the grove and all that. Hope to get my schedule all set so we can bullshit again in the lounge."

"Looking forward to that, buddy" Gary responded, patting him on the shoulder and converying a bond of personal and professional admiration. "See you soon. Welcome back" and Gary Carson turned left towards the surgical suites. Frank stood motionless for a few seconds, staring at the doors to that suite. Then the cloud reappeared. The fucking black cloud. A chill went up his spine and his pulse quickened again. "What the shit" he whispered to himself, "what the shit"

But as he entered the elevator and punched the button to his floor, the cloud seemed to float away. Alone, he felt relieved but concerned. Reaching his floor, he waited until the door opened, relieved again to see no one waiting. Turning left, he walked past the familiar scenes of his past life, hopefully to be his new past life again. Reaching the door of his office, he stopped for a moment to be certain his name was still on the door. Why, he thought, did I think it would not be? He grasped the handle firmly, opening the entry slowly and immediately the welcoming face of Helen, sitting behind her familiar desk, came into view.

"Dr. Martin!" she loudly exclaimed. "Welcome back! It seems yiou've been gone for weeks. Did you have as good a time as you had hoped?"

Smiling, Frank answered her quickly. "Better, Helen. It was terrific. But so good to see you." "I was busier than I thought, Doctor. Lots of calls. You have a full schedule this morning."

Why that sounded both reassuring and jarring he wasn't sure. He walked to her, gave her a quick kiss on her cheek, and asked to see the schedule. Sure enough, all the slots were filled. Three new consults to start things off.

After thanking her for complimenting him on his tanned skin, he moved into the office. There is always something comforting about familiar surroundings. It reinforces your sense of proportion. He glanced at the plaques that covered the west wall. His diploma from his undergraduate days, from his medical school and finally those from his post graduate training. He studied them each, as if to cement who he was. Strange. And, still, like a pulsating demon that black cloud would slip; in and out of his consciousness. He donned his white lab coat that was neatly hung on the back of his door. He still wore t, feeling it still projected an image of professionalism. Not all of his colleagues did any more, some feeling it made them appear too elite and removed. Maybe something to that but he had not stopped yet. With his newly acquired tanned skin coalescing with his white coat, his handsome features were magnified, apparent to him when Helen gave him a longer look than was customary. She handed him the information on his first patient, a middle-aged woman sent for consideration of aortic valve replacement. What was the word that was used? 'deja-vu?' Memories of the last middle-aged woman with an aortic valve malfunction. The infamous or famous Harriet Johnson, whatever it was. Well, sooner or later, Mr deja-vu would be here and now was that time. Face it. With more confidence than he thought he could muster, he opened the door and saw a slightly obese woman with wide eyes and hair thrown up in a pony-tail which he thought was unusual for this age. She was rather attractive though, her visage shining through her slightly plump background. Her name was Elizabeth Miller and she was sixty-three years old.

Walking in and introducing himself with a handshake, as firmly as he had offered in the past, she glanced up and, as frequently happened with his female patients, seemed to do a double-take, stunned, perhaps, by the sheer power of his good looks.

"Well, Mrs. Miller, let's find out why Dr. Grange asked you to see me"

Phil Grange was another of his cardiology friends who frequently referred the surgical cases to him and he found it reassuring that it seemed to be the case.

He went through the history rather quickly. It was fairly routine, the valvular dysfunction reaching the point where her functioning was affected with increasing shortness of breath and other signs of inadequate cardiac output. Very similar to that of Harriet Johnson.

"And did Dr. Grange suggest you may need a valve replacement?"

"Yes, he did. To tell you the truth, it scares me to death to think of that kind of surgery. But… but I am having more and more trouble breathing and, well, I guess I need to not be so afraid."

"I can't say I blame you. It is scary but much safer now. The techniques and materials are so much more advanced than just a few years ago."

"SO I have been told."

"Well, let's have a listen, should we?" he told her as he motioned her to get up upon the examining table. She offered no resistance as he pulled her gown apart to expose her chest. Women's breasts, in a clinical setting, had become routine and while he noticed he ignored for the most part. Mrs. Wilson's breasts were rather large, befitting her size he surmised, but he went on to listen to the heart sounds and the typical woosh of tightening of the aortic valve, like the current of a river oscillating against a dam.

Finishing, she climbed back off of the table, smiling at him, and took the seat next to his little examing room desk.

"Well, doctor, what's the verdict?"

"Nothing surprising. Yes, you certainly do have an abnormal aortic valve and yes, replacement is an option."

"Any other options?"

"TO do as you have been doing. Medical treatment."

"Ain't doing it" she responded half-heartedly, letting her head drop a bit to reflect her awareness of the obvious.

"DO I need to talk to your husband?" Frank asked innocently.

"I am a widow, Doctor. Doesn't your record show that?"

He felt embarrassed and speechless. Yes, the record did show that but he simply hadn't noticed.

'I'm sorry, Mrs. Miller. I didn't look carefully enough."

"Well, that really isn't a problem. My problem is what is the problem, not whether you looked at my record."

Franks sensed this was a different woman than Harriet Johnson, thank God. But why should that make a difference? He was sure that would never happen again.

She seemed to be her 'own woman' he surmised and so she planned the next move. Yes, she would have the replacement. She was certain that was what was needed and she gained more confidence as they continued to talk. His personal bedside manner, always important to him, along with his handsomeness gave her comfort. In the end, a date was set with Helen doing the schedulilng.

CHAPTER TWENTY FIVE

He slid through the remainder of the day rather easily, seeing several patients on simple follow-up and several new consults, two of whom also would require surgery but neither left the impression on him generated by Elizabeth Miller. It was as if Harriet Johnson had returned seeking his opinion again. Weird in some respects, not totally surprising in others. As he finished seeing his final patient, who happened to be a follow-up doing very well, he walked over to Helen who was beaming, her day once again a potpourri of scheduling, answering questions not needing his input, and all of the mechanical necessities of an office. "Well, Dr. Martin, how did this first day back feel?"

"Good, Helen. Not bad at all. Did you get the feeling that Elizabeth Miller had been in this office before?"

"I… not really. How do you mean?"

"She brought back memories. Memories of Harriet Johnson."

Greeted with a moment of silence, Frank was uncertain if he needed to say any more but she interjected her thoughts:" Well, now that you mention it, there is a bit of similarity isn't there? About the same age, basically the same problem. Does that bother you?"

"A bit, Helen. I must admit. But it also gives me the impression that it is what I needed."

She nodded at him, fully aware of all that had transpired and its effects on all connected to that case.

"Are we done for the day, Helen?"

"Yes we are, Dr Martin. A full day I must admit." "Are you ready to leave? It is a bit late?"

"I have just a few items to finish and then I'll be gone. And you?"

"I do not have anybody in the hospital so, yes, just a few notes to make and I can skeedadle back home."

And so it went. Alone in his office, he sat silently in his chair, looking about at the artifacts that covered his wall. Was Elizabeth Miller really what he needed? Had that black cloud drifted away? He just wasn't sure.

Disappearing beyond the horizon, the sun's glare ws a bit of a problem as he drove towards home that evening. In general, he felt secure about the situation and was prepared to do what he always did. He began to look forward to Elizabeth Miller's surgery, the template for the next phase of his medical life. He shard all of that with Carole and his children that evening at dinner, a somewhat rare treat for them all, at least that early hour. with his lack of need to return to the hospital prior to returning home.

"Daddy, how did it feel to be back in the office aftr your vacation?" Teri innocently asked.

"Good, sweetheart. I had a great day, really. Busy." "Is that good, I mean being busy?"

"Yes, Busy is good"

That brought laughter from Carole its infectiousness spread to the other three as they went through the meal with ease and joviality.

Later that night, after the children had turned their lights out and he was alone with Carole in their bed, he told her abut Elizabeth Miller and her eerie incarnation of Harriet Johnson.

"Really? Did she remind you of her?" "Yes. She really did.": 'Is that bothering you?" "No, I don't think so."

She wrapped herself around him, noting his firmness and he feeling the warmth and nearness of hr body

"Well, it shouldn't. My knight in shining armor will conquer all, including me."

They embraced passionately but quietly, having learned how to have sex even when they were not sure if Teri and Tim were still awake. He removed her gown quickly and felt her breasts pushing against him. Her hand went to his penis and then her mouth as they seemed to continue their island adventure in Chicago.

He slept well that night, awakening with the alarm but going about his business, as always, quietly and in semi-darkness. His breakfast, as always, was a cup of coffee, juice and, whole wheat toast. Occasionally, he added some cold cereal but not today as he found himself anxious to get to the hospital. There were only two cases for him, both relatively minor peripheral vascular stuff but still, surgery and for some reason, it excited him. Leaving before anyone else was awake, he drove comfortably that morning, electing to listen to music on his satellite radio rather than the usual nondescript talk shows.

Welcoming him back into the surgical sea, he could sense no doubts or apprehension from those immersed in that world. He felt at ease and confident. The younger nurses, always conscious of his sexuality, seemed more aware with his newly acquired tan and post-vacation demeanor. His surgical resident, aware of but mostly oblivious to the Ken Laser saga again appeared eager to learn and seemed appreciative of his skills which were well demonstrated but not challenged with these relatively easy procedures that morning. All in all, he felt that the black cloud had taken a vacation and hopefully, would never return. But he was mistaken.

It was not an unusual morning, that morning in which the surgery for Elizabeth Miller was scheduled. Approaching the middle of November, the skies over Chicago assumed their predictable gray shield with the winds doing their subtle but definite northward shift to announce the arrival of a new season. Frank sometimes welcomed this clarion call of nature, asking him to be more content to be within the confines of the walls of the hospital and doing what he did well, But he did admit to himself that he seemed not to tolerate the cold as he did as a youth.

Scheduled as the first patient in a busy surgical schedule pleased him. In general, he preferred to start early when the promise of the day was still carried on the rising beams of the sun.

Robert Hanson was his anesthesiologist, one of his favorites, steady and totally reliable. Martha Caraway, his scrub nurse, with him on many of his valve cases also reliable. His new resident, Mark Temple, was almost as good as Ken Laser and a bit more personable. Satisfying, that.

As was his habit, he always attempted to see his patient before the onset of the procedure, even if for a moment or two. The caring part of surgery, that part that could be conveyed only by the very human person to person contact, was to him as important as the technicalities. And so that morning in November, Frank went to greet Elizabeth Miller as she lay on the gurney. Reaching out to touch her hand, he asked her warmly:" And, are you ready to take care of this ridiculous little valve that is such a pain in you know what?" His smile was full and honest, conveying his appreciation of the importance of this to that person who would undergo the procedure and the need for them to place utter and total confidence in the entire team, but particularly the surgeon. Suddenly that thought sent a chill through him that he had not felt in weeks and the black cloud seemed to be over him again.

What the fuck! It was gone, for Christ's sake and now... His thoughts were interrupted by the pleasant response of Elizabeth Miller.

"Yes, certainly. I want to fix that little bugger." exhibiting her smile to match his. They held hands for the briefest of moments but enough for her to sense his genuine concern and to cement, even more, her trust in him. Frank could always sense that and had always taken additional confidence from it. But not today. Why not today? Was this not Elizabeth Miller and not Harriet Johnson? But he did what was necessary to hide these sudden surges of unwelcome emotions and their parting remained palpably pleasant.

He went through his usual preoperative preparation, the scrubbing of the hands, the donning of the gloves and the masks. He moved into the operating theater, the bright lights shining above him as familiar as the sun, the sterility of the whole place appropriate for what was to be done, the appearance of the nurses, of Robert Hanson, looking like explorers in the space of human anatomy.

"Everything is in order, Dr. Martin" Martha reassured him as Robert nodded in agreement as he took his position at the head of he operating table. Everything so familiar, so reassuring, so suited to the art of surgery. But for some reason, it just did not seem right. What was the matter? What the hell was the matter. But he was able to set aside these little waves of, what seemed to be doubt, as Elizabeth Miller was wheeled into that room, now the center of all it was. It's raison d' etre. In a matter of minutes, Robert Hanson had performed his magic, sending the arrows of unconsciousness straight to Elizabeth Miller, rendering her as putty in all of their hands. Such is the responsibility of all in that room and it seemed more so to Frank than it had in any of the cases he had faced since his return from St Vincent's. Making the incision into the chest seemed routine and went smoothly, as did the initial entry into the inner workings of that magnificent pump we call the heart. But then it happened. The black cloud seemed to come crashing into his head, the always steady hands not so now, the fear of a mistake seemingly overwhelming him. Fixing her eyes on him, Martha seemed stunned and confused. What was happening? It seems as if he is frozen. This is not our Dr. Martin.

"Dr. Martin. Are you all right?" she alarmingly asked.

"I… don't know. Jesus, I don't know, Martha."

"Can I help you, Dr. Martin?" Mark Temple quickly interspersed.

"I'll be fine. I just had a moment of deja vu. Harriet Johnson and all that, you know. Happens. Bob, all steady?"

"Fine, Frank. All vitals stable and level being well maintained." "Good. Let's get on with it."

Long after the operation on Elizabeth Miller, he still was not sure how he managed to complete that procedure. His head was filled with great waves of guilt and repeated image of Ken Laser. It may well have been the skills of Mark Temple in the assist that guided him through to the end and, he still never was sure how everything turned out as it did, but it did and the valve replacement was successful, the time consumed just about what was to be expected.

As he removed his glove in the surgery lounge, he could not help but notice how wet they were, the beads of perspiration had oozed into them. Not since his first few operations as a resident had this happened to him and he was frightened. Sitting in a nearby chair, he felt broken, the wall of confidence that every surgeon must maintain had been breached and he had a terrible foreboding that he might be finished. He had never contemplated that the death of Ken Laser and all that surrounded it would affect him quite like this. Would he be able to conquer this and return to that era when he really did feel as if he was the best cardiovascular surgeon in the city of Chicago. God, what if he could not? Oh my God, what if he could not?

Suddenly, the voice of Robert Hanson broke into his black reverie. "Frank. Are you all right? Never seen you freeze like that."

"I think so, Bob. I... you know, Ken's suicide really got to me, more so than I thought."

"Well, I can understand that. He was a great guy. Stunned all of us. No one expected a malpractice suit to do that to him or to any other doctor I guess." "I know keep hearing that being sued is just the 'price of doing business' But what it did to him was a fucking tragedy. A real tragedy." But deep inside, Frank knew it was more than just the suit itself. It was the feeling that Ken must have had of being 'framed' if you will.

"Frank, you know, as the saying goes,' time heals all'. Even this."

"I'm counting on that, Bob. But this one seems to be harder than I thought." "Look, I've known you long enough now to say with utter confidence, that will heal this for you too. Incidentally, how is that woman doing? What was her name, now?"

"Johnson, Harriet Johnson. As far as I know,. About the same. Neurologically compromised but… alive. Haven't really checked for awhile but now that you asked, maybe I need to."

He patted Frank on the shoulder as he got up to leave." On to the next triumph. Nice job on that valve. Good to see you again, as always, Frank." "Thanks. See you Bob. Always nice to work with an gas man like you." Robert Hanson nodded, a smile covering his rugged face, reinforcing what he also thought of himself, and he made his way to the next operating suite.

There was another case in about an hour but first he needed to step out to the lounge and tell Elizabeth Miller's niece how things went. Finding his way out the door and walking to the waiting areas, he noticed that his mouth was quite dry. Unusual. Anxiety? Doubt about the next case? What if he froze again? A surgeon cannot do that.

Elizabeth Miller's niece was a very attractive blonde in her thirties, Frank guessed. She was with her husband, he surmised. Or maybe her 'significant other" Introducing himself with a solid handshake to both, he reassured them that all went well and her aunt should be in the cardiovascular recovery area in a matter of an hour or two and they could hopefully visit her then.

"Thank you, Doctor" said her niece whose name was Linda." Aunt Liz had a lot of confidence in you."
"She is a very easy patient to work with. I am so glad I was able to help her She will be able to enjoy life better now, I assure you.
After a few more words, he turned And walked back towards the surgical lounge. The niece's words about confidence still vibrating through his head. The talisman of a surgeon, he knew. That confidence based on a variety of things, not least the air of total command you are able to convey. What if he lost that? What if he had already lost that? He could not deliberate on this forever, the next procedure, an aortic aneurysm repair, was coming up.
While not as involved and demanding as a valve repair, it needed complete concentration and that seemed to becoming a challenge for the first time in his professional life. The unwinding of his persona was, to say the least, quite troubling and he was not certain of the ultimate outcome As he prepared, he met several of his colleagues going about their business. He was able to interact as if nothing new was occurring, as if the same old Frank Martin, the top-notch cardiovascular surgeon was in total command, as always. Entering the operating room, he was able to comfort and reassure the patient, a middle -aged man who was not symptomatic but whose aorta had grown

too large for his primary care physician to ignore and so he was here, in Frank's hands. Mark Temple was waiting, no worse for the wear of the previous case gowned and mask in place, seemingly as capable as Ken Laser but... alive. When all was ready, the incision in the abdomen was made, easily and with little effort. As the aorta and its ballooning surface came into view, that strange feeling again came over him. Ken's face passed before him, quickly but too distinct to ignore. He once again seemed frozen in time, incapable of continuing. Knowing Mark could complete this one just as well as he, he moved back and told all those in the room that he did not feel well and he would just stand by. Years later, he still could not accurately describe the waves of emotion that cascaded through him at that moment in time. Convinced he was through as a surgeon, he stood frozen and terrorized, a trembling inside that overcame him to the point of total surrender.

Driving home that night after the day was complete, needing to cancel the third and final surgery, blaming his health as the reason, he was if in another world. He had never felt this way before. Panic was not quite the correct description of his state of mind. It was confusion and a bit of disorientation. He was convinced he would need to seek psychiatric help on this. What would that do to his reputation as a surgeon? In the new world, maybe nothing, but he was still frightened. Stopping the car a block short of his home, he sat for a period of time and tried to sort all of this out. How to tell Carole. How to react to his children's obvious question and concerns in a way they could understand.

Well, if this is the end of his life as he had known it, so be it, But what to do… well, maybe he was jumping a bit ahead of himself. Restarting the car, he slowly put it into drive and with melancholy and a degree of fear, inched his way the last few yards to his driveway.

Carol, as was her wont, greeted him shortly after he opened the door. Her beautiful, smiling face always lifted him, even now in this his hour of darkness.

"Hi Honey" she told him in her usual cheerful but always welcomed salutation. "How did this day of surgery go?" She did not expect what followed. Sitting her down in a kitchen chair, he went in detail about the events of the day and how he was frightened by their implications. He was not sure what his next step should be. For the first time, Carole comprehended the full impact of both that suit and the consequent suicide of Ken Laser on him and how it may well be slowly destroying that once invincible shield of competence and confidence.

"What to you plan to do?" She asked in a mixture of spousal concern and genuine fear.

"I'm not sure. I am just not sure. I… really am not certain I can do any more surgery at this point. Not if I feel like I did today."

"Have you thought about psychological assistance, Frank? That may help."

"Yes, I have. I do know a very good psychiatrist and I think you do too. Harold Siegel."

"Of course. I've talked to him on a number of social occasions and he seems such a nice person. Do you think he is as good professionally as he seems socially?"

"I guess I'll find out."

She embraced him with a passion that was welcomed, giving him that splinter of support that he would certainly need.

That evening, dinner was as somber as he could remember, Both Teri and Tim again were surprised that they were eating as early as they did, with their father often either absent or much later. Beginning with their usual exchanges that bound them together, he slowly inched into the story of his day. Tim seemed to understand what he was telling them better than Teri. Understood that their father was telling them that in essence, he might be a broken man, his ego shattered by what the death of a young associate had done to him Even at his age, he seemed to recognize the implications. Gloom. It was gloom now that settled over that table as even Terri joined in the recognition.
"Well, kids, don't be that upset. There is always light at the end of the tunnel. And there will be here. I'm going to talk to a few people who are knowledgeable about these things and we'll move on. "But all three of them recognized the lack of conviction in his voice, the uncertainty and the despair.

And so it was that Frank called and made an appointment with Dr. Harry Siegel the first thing that next morning.

CHAPTER TWENTY SIX

Having met Harry Siegel on several occasions, he had mixed feelings. Probably as solid as you might find in a psychiatrist, Harry had assumed the head of the Department about five years ago. In his mid-fifties, short but very athletic appearing, he had the reputation of being rather warm and cordial. Married to a beautiful woman half his age, he had made his mark on the social chambers of the hospital's Chicago scene, one of those people whose photo you can always find with his arms around some one or some two or three smiling at the camera at one function or another, usually self-conscious of his need to stand out next to those who towered above him. But, he was good. It was said he was very, very good at what he did.

His office was on the ninth floor, just a few flights above the surgical suites. Perhaps he acted as the guardian of the scruples of their medical world. Frank had been very reluctant to even consider this visit. Its ramifications seemingly breaking down his anchors of self-confidence and as always, in the background, the stigma of seeing a psychiatrist, particularly if you were considered one of the best cardiovascular surgeons in the City, unbreakable in every way.

But Carole had insisted he do this. For him, for her, for their children. She did not want to see his career destroyed by what a young, unstable resident had decided to do when faced with a disappointment. So, Frank entered the office of Dr Harry Siegel. He had lost all pretense of camouflaging who he was, all pretense that he could banish the demons on his own.

"Good morning" his receptionist cheerfully greeted him, knowing full well who he was. "Good morning. I am Dr Frank Martin and I have an appointment with Dr Siegel."
"Yes, I know, doctor. You are the first on his schedule and he wanted me to take you directly back to his office so you would not feel so uncomfortable being exposed in the waiting room'
Frank thought this was a bit melodramatic and protective, even a bit weird but, silently, he appreciated the gesture. He had decided to stay within the confines of his own medical world and he, was after all, not a stranger to those who inhabited it.

His receptionist, tall with full blonde hair and a buxom figure, seemed to fit into this space. The worldly Dr Siegel, unconventional but deeply rooted in his objectives.
She led him back into a matrix of rooms, staying just far enough ahead of him so he could, if this was the correct word, admire her posterior. His libido had been somewhat muted over the past few weeks and while he welcomed this mild awakening, she could not hold a candle to Carole.

Entering a rather cavernous office, wood-paneled and lined with photographs of whoever, it presented an impressive introduction for any patient. Sitting behind an equally space taking wooden desk sat Harry Siegel. Short, stout but cheerful and with a pleasant demeanor and seemingly untouched by any flaws he could detect, he stood up to shake Frank's hand.

"Dr Martin. Your fame precedes your visit. Please sit down. Thank you, Penny" he motioned to his assistant as she smiled once more at Frank and closed the door. "Please call me Frank."

"Ah yes. And me, Harry. Good. Now, I know it always takes some degree of courage for a fellow physician to see any psychiatrist. So, let's cut to the quick. Tell me your story."

So it began. Frank went through the litany from the first visit with Harriet Johnson to now. Finished, he watched as Harry Siegel arose from his chair and walked around the room, glancing a the photos that lined the walls. Strange, this diminutive figure, doing whatever this was meant to do. Perhaps this was the way he sorted his thoughts, meshing whatever psychiatrists mesh to arrive at an answer. After circling the room, pirouetting as it was, he sat back down, looked up at the ceiling, and finally spoke to Frank.

"This sort of thing has happened to a number of surgeons. You re not the first, Frank" "I did not imagine I was. So, what do I do or what do we do?"

Frank thought he detected a developing smile on his well tanned face.

"To regain your confidence, you must regain your confidence." What the fuck did he mean? Talking in riddles may not do it.

"I don't understand."

"Frank, I cannot, no one but yourself can get that confidence back. You know you are dealing with that blanket of guilt that you are directly responsible for Ken Laser's death You are not. I do not know why that happened to him. But something was not in place that should have been. Even if he was not in anyway responsible, it might have happened anyway. So, you need to work through that. Look what I am trying to say is that it is not usual for someone to commit suicide based on one issue alone. Yes, it may well be the catalyst but it is the tragic conclusion of a train of events that ultimately leads to that moment in time when there seemingly is no other way out. Usually, this is associated with depression. I did not know Ken Laser and admittedly this is a generalization but one that usually rings true. You're a very smart guy, Frank. This, then, is not an intellectual exercise but a battle where you are battling the windmills of emotional turmoil, obviously. You alone are not responsible for what happened. Period. Now we can spend many hours working our way through this but I have a feeling, from all that I have heard about you that you can handle this on your own. Ultimately, of course, that is the point of seeing me in this first place."

So that was it. It was up to him… Period. No shock to that. So be it. I'll get on with it. "I got the message, Harry. It's all in my court now."
"Yes, but if you ever have any questions or need any help in my department, you know I will be available at any time"
And so that was that. Intuitively, of course, he knew that this was the ultimate answer he would hear, But Harry was being quite honest.

"What I would like you to do is get back to the job you were cut out to do. Again, my listening posts have certainly confirmed that you are certainly one of the finest cardiovascular surgeons in Chicago, if not the state and who knows, the country. We should not lose that gift because you feel responsible for something for which you are absolutely not. Ken Laser would feel the same way as I"

All of this percolated within Frank's brain. Wave after wave of those conflicting thoughts again. Enormous pride about what Harry Siegel had so kindly said about him, the desire to resume doing what he knew he was so good at, but the black cloud seemed to still be there. No, he probably was not responsible for Ken's suicide but could he remove that shroud that hovered over him? While he was spiritual in a secular humanistic mode, he was not supernaturally religious and would not turn to a minister. Some would obviously, but not him.

Arising from his chair, still a bit unsettled, Frank shook Harry Siegel's hand.

"Thanks Harry. I appreciate your honesty. Of course, you are right. I guess psychoanalysis will not be the answer, after all."

With that, Harry Laughed as he arose to return the salutation. "NO, not really. But I am here for you, Frank.".

And so, he walked through the reception room, still empty, past his assistant whose eyes were targeted at him with a 'come hither' look which he returned with a smile, went out the door, took a deep sigh, and was determined to get on with his life.

CHAPTER TWENTY SEVEN

The months that followed his visit with Harry Siegel were fateful. He had communicated to Carole the short content of that meeting, expressing his mild surprise and amusement of the advice he had received although it did make eminent sense in the long run. His wife, also a bit surprised at the conclusion Harry Siegel had made, but since she did not want to draw this out, in the end agreed it simply was up to him 'getting that confidence back' But as time went on, he could not. He just could not.

His surgical colleagues noticed. The scrub nurses noticed. The residents noticed. He noticed. When the notice from Karl Green arrived in his hospital in-box, it did not surprise him. Whomever had noticed the most had informed Karl. Maybe more than one had informed him.
While he knew that day would come, it was still somewhat of as shock. He had never been summoned to the 'principal's office' in his life. Ever. In grade school, in high school, in college, in medical school. Never.

Calling Karl Green's office, he scheduled his appointment the next day, following his last surgery. His schedule had lightened a bit which added to his uneasiness.

Carole, too, had noticed the change and was growing ever more concerned. Their personal relationship was suffering a bit, his usual gregariousness replaced by a more sedate and introverted disposition.

"Honey" she implored, "can you get on top of this?"

"God, I just do not know. I just don't know. I never, never thought Harriet Johnson would possibly lead to all of this bullshit. Never. The fucking suit, the suicide of Ken and… now, now it has taken me over. I am not the surgeon I used to be."

Those words seared her like a burning arrow. Right to her heart. These were the words of surrender, she knew it. Maybe he needed a leave of absence. Something. The island vacation just did not do it. What would?

"So where do we go now?"

"I don't know. Maybe my surgical career is finished."

"Frank! Goddamn it, don't ever say that again. Ever. You are just too talented to leave it. It'll get better, baby, I promise"

She moved over to embrace him, her compassion wrapped in sadness and despair. For the first time in their marriage, she harbored doubts about the success of her husband. How could that lawsuit, that, what did they say about malpractice, it's just 'the price of doing business' undo and destroy him as she was now witnessing? She had known wives of other surgeons who also had been sued but she could not recall anything like this. Sure, it took a few a while to get their bearings back, to regain their equilibrium, but this? This?

"What to you think this visit to Karl is all about?"

"My inadequacies. My slide down the slippery slope. What else could it be?"

His eyes clouded over with that look of resignation, as if he was certain of the eventual outcome of all of these issues.

"Well, you just tell Karl that it will just take a little more time and Dr. Frank Martin will be on top of it all once again. Just a little more time."

She embraced him again, their lips meeting in a kiss now bearing the imprimatur of more hope than certainty. But that night, still wrapped in his cloud of despair, Carole did her feminine best to clear it from him, if only temporarily. The power of sex to heal can be powerful if the circumstances are just right. They were not. All of the incredible libido he had displayed in St Vincent's seemed to have evaporated since their return. Her disappointment and concern was grave. He was obviously becoming more depressed about this. He was adamant about not using anti depressants and she did not press him.

The meeting with Karl Green did not go well. Concern was raised about Frank's performance or, better, his lack of performance over the past several months.

"I simply cannot understand this at all, Frank" Karl righteously purveyed to him after outlining the summary of the reports he had received." You are, or shall we say, you were the best goddamn cardio surgeon in this hospital. Maybe in all of Chicago. Maybe in the whole state of Illinois. What the fuck happened ?"

Frank was now used to the waves of regret those words would bring to him. His answers had flowed to meet the circumstances, chameleon-like.

"I cannot explain it all, Karl. Since the lawsuit and Ken Laser's suicide, it is as if this black cloud has settled over me, like an ephemeral hand that just crushes my confidence. I cannot shake it. And yes, I did see a psychiatrist." His voice was subdued, surrendering, abject. Karl Green, no idiot, recognized the tones of a man defeated. He was both stunned and sad, unable to pick the right words to describe his utter disappointment and feeling of loss for the talent that sat before him

"Well, Frank. I am utterly speechless. I don't know what more to add. I am going to have to ask you to take a leave of absence until you get that black cloud out of the way. I really think you will. And I hope you will. I just hate to see that operating room without you. I honestly do. Take all of the time you need. Do you have enough funds to get you through this?"

"Yes. I think so." Although that thought, while having being considered, now was a reality. "Thanks, Karl, for your kind words. I'll let you know when I feel more comfortable with myself"

He stood up, reached over to shake Karl Green's hand, noticing the extra firmness Karl seemed to project, turned and walked out of the office, officially no longer a functioning member of the surgical staff, in a no man's land, in a desert with no visible oasis. A man lost.

Dropping by his office, he felt as if his world had collapsed, as indeed it seemed to have. There sat Helen, the rock of his former hospital life, busy doing God knows what. Seeing him, she stopped and put whomever she was talking to on apparent hold, to greet him.

"Dr. Martin. I didn't expect to see you so soon this morning. You do have a case in twenty minutes you know."
Actually, he had forgotten that he had. Fortunately, or unfortunately, he didn't know how to judge it, it was his only case of this light day. He suspected he needed to do it,

of course, and he would. But first, to Helen. "Yes, I know. Helen, do me a favor?"

"Of course."

"Don't schedule any further office patients."

"Any? Starting when? Are you going on another vacation?' Had she no insight into what had been going on for the past several months? Maybe not. Maybe not.

Her face projected the visage of innocence and bewilderment intertwined in a question.

"Just don't schedule any starting now. I'll be back after I finish this case."

"Why, yes, Dr. Martin. I'll stop now. Is something wrong?"

"I'll talk to you more after I return."

"Fine. I hope there is not. See you soon."

Unable to cancel this seemingly 'last case', he strode into the surgeon's lounge with as much manufactured confidence as he could muster. He had come to terms with the 'black cloud': so I cannot shake you, I'll do my best to do my best under you. One more time, just one more time. Harry Kahn was there, sitting in a straight- backed chair, calmly reading the Chicago Tribune, dressed in his greens, the quintessential portrait of a surgeon readying to do battle. God, those were the days, he thought.

"Frank!" Harry blurted as soon as he spotted him. "How goes it?"

Did he know what he thought every surgeon on this staff knew? That ol' Frank ain't what he used to be?

"It goes well, Harry. And you?" he answered in as cheerful a voice as he could muster.

"Well, Frank, well. What are you up to this morning?"

"Bypass. Two blockers." He gave the reigning jargon for

a coronary artery bypass involving two blocked arteries. "And you?"

"A young woman with a small mass in her kidney.

Probably malignant but will do the frozen ands see how far we need to go."

And so the 'shop talk' went on. The medical parlance that shaped their professional lives, the grammatical rhythm that he knew he would sorely miss.

Dressing in his uniform at his locker, he thought for what might be the last time. Ever. Ever. Goddamn that black cloud, goddamn Harriet Johnson, goddamn Ken Laser! He wanted to cry. Just sit down and cry. A lifetime of work soon to end. Doing the ultimate in what one human can do to change the life, positively, of another human. Would he never have that indescribable feeling again ? Closing up after surgery, certain that a job well done had been completed, looking forward to meeting the patient, meeting the family, and sharing in their joy, and if the unthinkable happened, helping them cope with the unthinkable. One more time, Frank, he thought. Do the best fucking job you can do here. The best.

And so he finished his preliminary preparation, entering the operating room, the familiar glare of the lights capturing him as he held out his hands for the scrub nurse to help him into his gloves, nodding to Mark Temple, relaying the words of confidence, such as they were, to the patient, a middle-aged man who was otherwise in excellent health, watching as the anesthesiologist started the flow of the magic dust that would render him totally inert. He was in his hands now, black cloud or no black cloud. Taking the scalpel, he boldly made the incision that would lead to the separation of the sternum, Mark Temple and a nurse applying the instrument to spread the ribs, inching slowly but carefully to that throbbing ball that is the heart, identifying the blocked arteries and preparing to harvest the veins from his leg to bypass them. All went well. Was it the fact that he knew it had to go well, that he could do just one more of these under that cloud, the thought of not needing to do it again that guided him to the end, watching with satisfaction, with that old glory-filled satisfaction as Mark Temple closed the chest wound. And so it was done. Would he ever do this again?

"Well done, Doctor Martin" the lead nurse offered him.

"Thank you Beverly" he answered.

"Good job, Mark" he told his resident as he took off his gloves and turned to leave the operating room, satisfied that he had indeed done a good job. But now what?

First. To see Helen. He assumed she was quite apprehensive about what he had told her and when he returned to his office, indeed, she was just that.

Sitting down in a chair next to her, in an empty office, with the noon sun darting in and out of the shadows as of his solitary window, he began: "Helen. I do not know if you have noticed anything in the past few months but since Ken Laser's death, I have had great trouble concentrating and doing the caliber of surgery I expect out of myself. This morning I was asked to see Dr Green. We had an amiable meeting but the long and short of it was that I was asked to take a leave of absence. I do not know how long that will be. I just don't. But, I think it best for me to close my office. No sense in paying rent and other overhead for nothing. I will help you find other employment and if I return I certainly will be in immediate contact with you." Feeling a sudden emptiness and regret, he awaited Helen's response.

Her usual calm visage, confident and mellow, masking her deceiving age of 60, now looked less so. He noted what he thought were a few tears starting to intermix with the mascara with that look of a woman in lament.

"I... don't know what to say, Dr Martin. Yes, I am aware of the stories going around about you." Pausing, she looked at the floor, then continued" but I don't believe them."

He smiled at her, connecting with that bond that humans form with one another, good or bad.

"Some are true. Helen, I think I do need to get away for a while, not just a short vacation but for awhile. I need to get my life back in repair, at least my professional life. I hope it will be soon. I do love what I do but I need to be certain I am doing it like it should be done. At this point, I am not so sure.

"I will miss you"

"And I you" he leaned over and gave her an unexpected kiss on her moistened cheek which unloosed a more ample flow of tears.

And so it went. He cleaned out his office, taking what he needed. The furniture was rental from the hospital so they would take care of that. He removed his diplomas and awards, found a box for them and placed them aside to be retrieved in a day or two when he and Carole would finally empty the remaining items. He dreaded telling Carole but he would do what he needed to do. Would he ever escape that black cloud? He did not know. But he needed to recharge and realign himself if he ever hoped to return to this place.

CHAPTER TWENTY EIGHT

And so he faced Carole and his children that night, after they both had returned from school. Tim, prescient as he had turned out to be, sensed a problem the moment he set his eyes upon him and in his typical uninhibited manner bluntly asked him what was the problem and why was he home so early.

"Tim, Teri, you both remember the trial I had and Dr Laser, don't you?"

Teri looked at him with too much innocence but quickly responded: "Yes"

"All of that has had an effect upon me. I think you know that already. But I haven't been able to perform at the level that I think a surgeon needs to perform to keep doing what he does."

"What does that mean, Dad?" Tim inquired with a bit of a frantic wisp in his voice.

"It means I closed my office today. Until further notice."

Immediate, not unexpected, tears from Teri, her young eyes welling with fluid, the dripping down her face, waiting to explode but yet able to exclaim in her childish innocence:

"You mean... you aren't a doctor anymore?"

Grinning, Frank told her no, he was still a doctor, just not a practicing one for now. He needed to sort things out and then could return to what he always did, and loved.

"And, when the school year is up I want to move. All of us to Arizona. Get away from this Mid-west cold and snow and start kind of new."

Even Carole was startled at that proclamation.

"Frank", she said in astonishment, "what is this all about?"

"I think a complete change of scenery will help. I will try to get a position in some area of medicine aside from surgery. For now."

He had been thinking of this for some time now, convinced he needed to leave the Chicago area so he would not be reminded of Harriet Johnson, Ken Laser, and the hospital that held so many memories for him, both good and bad.

"But Dad" Tim interjected "I like where we live. I like my school and my friends. Can't this all be sorted out here?"

"Maybe. But I think somewhere else would be a lot better for me. Both of you kids are outgoing, personable, and smart. You can adjust to anything, I am convinced. Besides, wouldn't it be nice to see all of those mountains and be outside most of the year without clouds, snow, ice, and all of that crap."

The conversation went on for a bit longer before he sensed some sort of acceptance by both of them. Carole had remained ominously silent during most of the discussion.

"Frank, I am still in a state of shock. You never hinted that this was your plan. Never."

A feeling of uneasiness crossed over him, pushing the black cloud aside for a moment.

"I know, honey. But can you see my point? I wanted to talk to you first but I thought I needed to make this more or less a family announcement, if you will." During the discussion, she had experienced a cornucopia of emotions. Yes, some of what he said did make sense but there was still the issue of Teri and Tim and their school and their friends, not to mention parents. But he was not going to do surgery for now, maybe for a long now, she knew that. This must be crushing him, she thought, just crushing him. The best damn cardia surgeon around and now, this. But if he needed a change of scenery to heal, so be it. He was her husband, for better or worse, and he was her hero, her friend, and lover, a living example of that old cliche. She knew how much he loved what he did and there had to be a chance he could do all of that again.

"All right, Frank. If this is what you think you need to do to heal, we will do it."

And so it went. The decision had been made. Now came the harder parts, the nuts and bolts of deciding to change the projectory of one's life. Should they sell or rent their home Would he ever return to Chicago? Where would they go in Arizona? His choice was Phoenix, Carole had not thought about it and the children were resigned to their fate. Where would he find a job, and in what, and did he need to get an Arizona license.? How would they break all of this to her parents, who, obviously would be heartbroken at their departure. But you do what you must do, he thought. It was just two months until the school session ended, so Frank and Carole decided to wait it out, to make it a bit easier on the children. It would be a bit difficult, he thought, but it may take that amount of time to sell the house and he would go to Phoenix to start exploring his options.

Over the next two weeks, they had met and discussed all of this with her parents. As they both suspected, it was a difficult message to convey. But, somewhat surprisingly, that decision was accepted but with great resignation, and the expressed hope that they would return to the Mid-west when Frank had restored his medical life to normalcy.

A month later, Frank boarded a plane at O'Hare on his way to Arizona.

CHAPTER TWENTY NINE

Taking one last look at the courtroom, he found his way to the exit, stepping, once again, into the chill of a Chicago early winter. Buttoning his coat, one that he rarely used any longer in Phoenix, he decided to drop by the hospital to say hello to Karl Green, if he was still there. He had been gone now for almost three years. Funny, he hadn't really communicated with any of his former colleagues, in spite of Carole's urgings to do so. Was it his attempt to block out that last few months, a sense of failure and embarrassment or just inertia? Maybe all three and maybe even other subconscious reasons. But he hadn't. He had, however, communicated with Ken Laser's family.

That atmosphere of resentment, even hate, seemed to have mellowed with time and they had come to accept the fact that the actual death of their son was not directly tied to Frank. But they certainly had not completely forgiven him, if that was the word one would use in this setting. Hailing a cab, he set out for the hospital, a bit uneasy but something he felt he needed to do, to undo the years of failing to speak with any of those with whom he had often worked so closely. As they drove down familiar streets, Frank quickly noticed the look of the city at this time of year. He had grown somewhat accustomed to the topography of the Southwest, even the desert with its constant sepia hue and the man made camouflage of green in the cities. Here, the trees were void of their leaves, the ground absent its green mantle of any kind, the skies overcast with the threat of snow. But the sights ushered in a flow of nostalgia and loss. Finally, the cab inched its way into the entry way of the hospital and the inanimate structure took on a character of its own to him. It was home, a workplace, full of memories of triumph and loss, of tears of both joy and sadness, and finally, where his life had been put on hold. Paying the cabbie, he walked slowly through the large, revolving doors that led to the main entrance. He wondered if he would recognize anyone behind that large wooden desk. He did not but the turnover at those positions was always rapid. Not expecting to see any physician he knew in this entry way, he entered the elevator along with a number of others and pushed the floor where Karl Green camped out. He really did not know if Karl would be in, not having set anything up in advance, but he would take his chances. As he walked into the office, he did recognize the receptionist behind the office desk.

Looking up, she immediately knew who he was.

"Dr Martin! What a pleasant surprise! It's been too long. So nice to see you. What brings you back to Chicago?"

"Bunch of little items I needed to take care of. I hope that Dr Green is around."

"As a matter of fact, he is in his office today. He is with one of the section heads now but please stay. I'll let him know you are here." "Thanks. I will."

Sitting in one of the office chairs, not really very comfortable but doable, he picked up one of the magazines on the table. It had to do with patients and surgeons. Thumbing through the pages, he found a few articles that seemed interesting and were, as he read through two of them. It brought back the nuts and bolts of the surgeon's craft, adding to the undercurrent of nostalgia he was feeling. He almost did not hear Rita's (as he now knew was her name) announcement that Dr Green would be delighted to see him now.

Stepping through the door of his office, Frank saw the familiar, albeit a bit older, visage looking up from some papers he walked in. His hair had grayed a bit more since they met last but the intensity of his eyes remained the same. He stood up quickly to greet Frank "Frank! What a wonderful and pleasant surprise. Thank goodness I was here, eh? Wouldn't want to miss seeing you. Please, sit down and tell me what the hell had been going on with you over the past… what? Three years."

"'Three" was Frank's laconic answer

He took one of the large chairs opposite Karl's rather large oak desk.

"Well, Karl, as you know, I closed my office here after our conversation. I was a bit tired of the Mid-west winters and had often fantasized about escaping it. Carole and I had vacationed a few times in Arizona and liked the change of topography and obviously the climate. So, after deciding to pack it up and go to Phoenix, I went out and found something to do before Carole and the kids came out. Besides, they wanted to finish the year of school here, which they did."

"Did you?"

"Well, I must admit, I looked for a bit. But I just didn't feel it could be in any surgical field, yet. But, I did not want to give up the patient contact. So, I eliminated any administrative ideas although I think I could have handled them and still might but at that time, I wasn't ready to do it. As you know, I have always felt the electricity between a patient and their doctor was special. Very special."

"I know" Karl answered, as if he had special access into Frank's inner musings.

"So, I finally took a position in the ER of the Veteran's Hospital."

"But didn't that involve some surgery?" "Yes but it is all very minor stuff that a first year resident could do. It was easier to dot the I's with the VA There wasn't much investigations about any malpractice but they did ask for some references. I'm surprised you didn't remember."

Karl looked slightly embarrassed for a moment.

"I guess I don't but I would not have said anything that would have prevented you from getting any medical work that didn't involved major surgery. But go on. How is that working out?"

"Not bad. I know just enough general medicine, or at least I did after a bit olf brushing up, to handle it and, obviously, any trauma is kind of up my alley. And, I can spend time with patients, without establishing any long term relationships with them. I still want to get back into cardio surgery, Karl"

Uncertain as to what the response would be, Frank watched the face opposite him for any tell tale signs. Surprisingly, it came rapidly.

"And you should. You are one of the best I have ever known."

Well, what do I do with that, Frank thought. "Thanks Karl I truly appreciate that."

223

"But are you ready, Frank? Has that, what do you call it, that "black cloud" drifted far enough away?"

"I don't know. I... think it might have. I feel comfortable when I go into the hospital every day. Confident and thinking I can still repair valves and do bypasses and all the other stuff'

"Would you consider returning here if that confidence stays?'

Frank knew he would be asked that question. He had thought about that more than once since he left Chicago. He had found Arizona more to his liking than he thought he would, even though he expected some of the benefits he was experiencing out West. Carole had settled in, obtained a marketing position at one of the up and coming firms. Both Teri and Tim adjusted much better than he imagined they would. Tim, particularly, was enjoying the change of scenery and did not seem to miss the Mid-western climate but did the change of seasons, particularly around Christmas.

"I don't know, Karl, honestly. You know how I loved this hospital and my colleagues in it. But, the memories, the reminders of the hell I went through, the tragedy of Ken, the very bad taste that suit left in my mouth. I think Chicago and the shadows it casts for me, even though this is my place of origin obviously, might keep that black cloud over me forever. I just don't know."

It was an honest answer. He knew that the fact he had been sued, the fact that Harriet Johnson had not even died, should never had disconnected him as it did. It had troubled him greatly that his self-image had been so utterly distorted and kept him from performing at the level he needed to perform those things that brought him such great satisfaction and fulfillment. Was it Ken's suicide that was the straw that broke the camel's back, so to speak, or something more? He did not know. He had visited another psychiatrist in Arizona and underwent a few sessions but even that did not do it all. Never a religious man, he knew he would not find the answers in theological spirituality. He had even talked several times with Alan Donnaldson, trying to get his take on malpractice suits and their effect on different physicians and how he fit in. Told that his reaction was 'unusual' he resigned himself to not seeking any further legal enlightenment. And so he sat here, in front of his former colleague and chief, without the answer Karl sought, as did he. "Well, Frank, you know you always welcome to return. I can only wish you the best of luck. And don't be so distant. Keep in touch, will you? Let me know how things are going. I continue to feel the world is being deprived of one its brightest surgical stars, I truly do." "Again, thanks Karl. Please say hello to Lillian for me. Your wife was always the sweetest thing. I'll keep in touch. Tell everyone that I am fine and healthy, and, who knows, maybe I'll see them here soon enough. In the meantime, if any of them, and you, are ever in Phoenix, give me a ring. Love to show you around. The desert and all that"

Both men stood and Karl walked around his desk and clasped Frank's hand firmly and pulled him closer for a genuine show of admiration. Frank fell a bit giddy, even tearful a the thought of what had been lost. Walking out of his door, through the waiting room, and down the elevator to the lobby where he found a cab. He would visit the parents, complete a few personal matters that required his attention, and finally go back to O'Hare for the flight to Phoenix and an uncertain destiny.